Why do books always leave

Well, I don't know! Go goog

Oh, lookie here. Another blank page.

Have you tried googling it yet?

I Have Three Toasters And Don't Toast Bread

I have three toasters and don't toast bread.

I've wondered if something is wrong with my head.

But something about them catches my eye,

As I walk by the counter where they're all piled high,

And I think to myself,

"Why, why, WHY?"

But I can't deny...

I have three toasters and don't toast bread.

And would you look at this? Blank! Except for the copyright stuff. What a waste of paper!

Copyright © 2022 by Violet Thorne and Lenore Thorne. All rights reserved.
59% of the writing by Violet Thorne
38% of the writing by Lenore Thorne
3% of the writing by Violet Thorne's alternate personality, "Vio"
Spelling and grammatical errors by Lenore Thorne
Constant criticism by Lenore Thorne
Cover Design by Violet Thorne because she's too poor to hire a professional designer
Drawings by Violet Thorne (except for the one on the front of this page which is by Gregory Thorne, aka Dad, and the last one in the book which is by Lenore Thorne, aka the co-author)
Edited by Violet Thorne because she's also too poor to hire a professional editor
Formatted by Violet Thorne
Footnotes by Violet Thorne because she just wanted to put in footnotes

CONTENTS

1: Rachel Convinces Her Friend Not To Destroy the Universe   1
2: Josh Vs. Human Interaction   7
3: Josh's Shopping Plan Is Defeated by an Extravert Friend   12
4: Learning From Mistakes Gone Wrong   18
5: Revisiting the Floating Toaster   25
6: Rachel Becomes an Honorary Member of the Bro Manly-Man Club   32
7: the Problem With Environmentally Friendly Buildings   37
8: Buying Mattresses From the Moon   44
9: Josh Decides "HI" Might Be a Nice Thing To Say   50
10: Playing Toaster Volleyball in the Cyber Void   54
11: the Painful Philosophy of Silly Putty   64
12: Mr. Knot Exhibits his Exceptional Observational Skills   68
13: Human Locomotion: The Ultimate Goal of Existence   78
14: the Science of Spontaneous Human Appearance   83
15: Restrictive Speed Limits Save the Economy   88
The Toaster Challenge   I
Untoasted: the Tragic Story of a Toaster Activist   V

What is this? Another blank page? WHY? I give up.

But seriously, you should google it…

For Grandpa Thorne
You always loved commenting on the installments I shared of this book while I was writing it. I wish I could give you a copy now that it's all done! We miss you.

It's finally beginning…

1: Rachel Convinces Her Friend Not to Destroy the Universe

> THE BOOKS I READ ARE ALWAYS DRY.
> IT SEEMS, ALTHOUGH I DON'T KNOW WHY,
> THE WET ONES TEAR AND MAKE A MESS,
> SO DRY BOOKS SEEM TO BE THE BEST!

No matter what some science fiction enthusiasts may imagine, Time never stands still. This is partially due to the fact that Time has neither feet nor legs on which to stand, and partially because if he did, he would always be running. However, instead of standing, or running, Time is forced to simply tick. Or fly, if people decide to have a good time, and allow the poor fellow some wings.

Granted, Time sometimes does drag out, and this is when things get rather miserable.

Of course, the speed of light has a great deal to do with all of this, but neither it, nor Time, nor most other people, understand this connection at all.

But, Time does not stand still.

Therefore, you should be well aware that the thoughts running through the head of the very ordinary Rachel Mew are, after all, quite incorrect. You might also be aware that referring to thoughts as "running" is odd, as most thoughts do somethings more like crawling, but we shall let it pass this time.

Rachel Mew is actually extraordinary. This is clear when you consider how many ordinary people there are, and then realize she is another one. There you have it: Rachel is extraordinary—she is an extra-ordinary.

It wasn't because she was any *less* special than anyone else. That would have made her less "extra." The problem was more that she was exactly as special as everyone else. So remember, when someone tells you you're a special person, but they also believe everyone's a special person, they're really saying you're a very average ordinary person. This is one case in which you can have it both ways—if everyone is special, then everyone is perfectly ordinary and un-special. Sad, but true. Or perhaps not so sad, since being special is overrated.

Rachel Mew rarely considered her state of ordinariness. She was far more concerned with her weight. You see, Rachel was under the impression the modern view of beauty was the correct one. She didn't realize had she lived a few hundred years earlier, she would have been considered quite breathtaking.

But as it was, "breathtaking" was more the effect running or going up stairs had on her. I'm afraid our dear Rachel Mew was rather overweight. It was quite sad for her really, because instead of just living her life and being happy, she was more concerned with starving herself to death and avoiding stairs.

I suppose, however, had she not been concerned with her weight, her status as an ordinary overweight young woman would have been in jeopardy.

Back to the thoughts in her head though—they were all quite incorrect.

She was reliving the moment in a romance movie when the two main characters, the ones who got married, walked into the room and saw each other for the first time. She was imagining at that exact moment, everything, even time itself, stood still.

She smiled dreamily, and then remembered the main female character had been slim and beautifully tanned. She sighed and shook her head, remembering her own pale and blotchy skin.

"It doesn't matter," she told herself, but while kind of objectively true, to her it was a lie. It did matter to her.

"I shouldn't watch romance movies," she told herself, but she knew she'd watch another one in a heartbeat—if the filmmaker didn't happen to make it longer than that.

Rachel Mew was dreadfully romantic, which, I'm afraid, was only ordinary. She also occasionally tried not to be, which was usual, and failed (even more common).

She also got dreadfully poor high-school grades, which was also ordinary for romantically-minded young people.

She was *not*, however, in a relationship of any kind, nor was likely to be in the near future. This was slightly unusual. It was the first glimmer of a nice difference in Rachel's life, as well as one of the things that made her most miserable.[1]

Whether Maria Higgins was more miserable than Rachel or not was hard to tell. However, it was clear that when the two were together, their mutual level of miserableness went down significantly.

If you were to compare Rachel to every other object in the universe and then to Maria Higgins, you would find them almost identical. However, if you were to compare them only to each other, you would find a good number of differences.

First of all, and most importantly, they were, in fact, different people. All the other differences are less critical to understand.

Maria Higgins was skinny, black, tall (Rachel was rather short), wore glasses because she was near-sighted, and was as little interested in romance as it was possible for her to be. And the little she was interested she tried much harder than Rachel to erase, and oddly, failed just as badly—if not worse. However, her failure in this area seemed to bother her a great deal more than Rachel's did her.

Maria was an odd young woman, and while odd in a very ordinary way, she was perhaps slightly less "extra" than Rachel.

---

[1] Not that Rachel Mew was really *most* miserable. There were plenty of people more miserable than her, as well as many who were less so.

Interestingly enough, Maria considered herself quite ordinary. She thought about this subject a good deal, and decided, considering the number of people in the universe, there must be countless others similar to herself. This will show you she is, after all, somewhat unusual, since most people don't think about their ordinariness at all, much less consider it in mathematical terms.

Maria Higgins liked many things—books, running, writing, goats, packed lunches, and much more—including a fondness for watching old TV shows.

This fondness brought together Maria Higgins and Rachel Mew. This, and the fact that they lived next door, and that when they had been kids their parents had been friends. Oh, and that a man was mowing his lawn one day and his lawnmower spit out a rock that flew into the road and hit a passing car, causing so much damage to the car it had to stop at a car repair shop in a town the car's drivers, Rachel's great-grandparents, fell in love with and moved to and therefore caused Rachel Mew to be born in the right place at the right time to meet Maria Higgins. And a great many other things as well that need not be mentioned here.

One day, when Rachel and Maria had just finished watching an old TV show together, Maria turned to Rachel and said quite unexpectedly, "hey Rach, I just had kind of an idea. Why don't we destroy the universe?"

Rachel stared at her for a full minute and then asked slowly, "Why?"

"Well, I figured all the stories are about people saving it, so why don't we get a little original for once?"

"The only reason there are so many stories of people trying saving the universe is because some other person is trying to destroy it. We would not be doing anything original at all."

"Oh, of course it wouldn't really work destroying it anyway. Someone or other would stop us and save it. But it might be kind of fun—and challenging. After all, no one's done it before."

"Mar, what on earth? You've been watching too many superhero movies, haven't you?"

"No, sci-fi. But I'm serious. Why don't we do something that people will actually remember for once?"

Rachel then felt it necessary to point out that if they destroyed the universe then no one would be left to remember them.[2]

"Oh, well," said Maria. "I still think it would be fun."

"Fun is exactly what it wouldn't be, unless you find being dead fun."

Miss Higgins laughed. "Think about it Rach, think about it."

"I already have! If you want to make a difference, why don't you go replant the rainforest or something?"

Rachel could see this suggestion didn't satisfy her friend at all, but could also see few suggestions would. She, however, was perfectly content imagining she was making a difference by doing absolutely nothing, and had very little desire to help Maria be satisfied.

---

[2] For this reason, destroying the universe is generally held to be a bad idea.

2: Josh vs. Human Interaction

> When people are boring they say boring things.
> But in summer and spring...
> They're the same as in winter and fall.
> They're boring! What did you expect?

P*eople. Boring people.*
   Josh flopped onto his bed. Ah, yes. I guess I'd better describe Josh. Josh was eighteen, with shaggy dark brown hair and skin that would have been brownish if he spent enough time outside to get even a slight tan.

Josh had just spent the better part of a day conversing with people, or more accurately, listening to other people converse. Human interaction usually had this flopping result for him, and today had been no exception.

He'd been interacting with other humans since his birth, but the task still seemed difficult and nearly always useless.

People had just run out of interesting things to talk about. Humans had reached the point where there was really nothing more that could be said that would be funny, or interesting, or helpful, or even worth listening to at all, for any reason whatsoever.

Annoyingly enough, most people did not recognize this. They just continued blabbing on and on. So, Josh had come to the conclusion that either everyone had short term memory loss and literally did not realize they never talked about anything that hadn't already been discussed...or they were delusional. He'd decided long ago he did not want to be either of those things, so he simply stopped talking altogether, unless absolutely necessary.

Unfortunately for Josh, other people did not understand why he didn't talk, and instead thought he was one of those introverts who did not like talking. This was not at all true. Josh would have dearly loved to have a nice, interesting conversation with someone, but that was impossible, because nothing was left for anyone to talk about.

He still remembered the day when the last new thing had been said. A friend of his had been taking about how she heated her soup up with a hair dryer. Then, that was it. The last original thing had been discussed; the next thing she said had already been said. Nothing anyone had said since had been new. The human race had run out of ideas.

Sadly, try has he might, Josh fared no better than the rest of them. And that was the ultimate reason he had flopped on his bed.

As he lay there staring up at the ceiling, he wondered if he would ever find anything interesting again. He probably would not. That was just his fate. Fate was so cruel.

Just then, one of the few people whose presence he occasionally tolerated walked into the room. It was Brandon, the blond guy who lived in the apartment room down the hallway.

Brandon watched him for a moment, and then pretended as if his bones had been made of string cheese, swaying for a moment and then flopping dramatically on top of him. Josh was crushed, in body and spirit. How dare his apartment neighbor not respect his personal boundaries?

"Hey! Get off," Josh gasped. He decided this was one of those few life and death moments when it was worth saying something even if 4.3 trillion people had already said it. His friend proceeded to slowly roll off of him until he was laying next to him on the bed.

"Hi," he said, and grinned.

Josh groaned. His friend couldn't have come up with a more overused word! "Hi," or some variant of a greeting, had been said by basically every human who had ever lived hundreds of times throughout their lives.

"You want to go for a hike? Everyone else is."

If he really wanted Josh to join him, saying everyone else was going was an extremely bad tactic. As if everyone else doing something was a good reason to do it, too! No thanks! Why couldn't anyone be original? Needless to say, Josh did not have much of a problem with peer pressure.

His friend sat up and stared at him for awhile. "I guess that's a no, Josh? You really should get out of the apartment more."

"Because everyone else is doing it? No thanks, I'll stay here. I don't pay rent so I can *not be in* my room." Too many overused words! His friend needed to leave, he was causing Josh to lose his resolve to stop adding to the boringness.

"Alrighty. Have a good time moping."

Brandon rolled off the bed and walked over to the doorway. He stopped and looked back at Josh. *No, do not say bye, do not!*

"Bye, Josh."

No!

He left. Josh breathed a sigh of relief. Now, he only had one boring human to deal with—himself. And it would be pretty miserable.

He looked over at the toaster.

Ah yes, the toaster: the toaster he'd moved into his bedroom and hung from the ceiling to prove that he could be original. He learned later his friend who warmed her soup with a hairdryer had already done the same thing. What a disappointment.

The toaster dangled there rather pitifully by its cord. Josh almost felt sorry for it. Maybe he should take it down. But then, he remembered that he'd told his friend he wouldn't take it down, and if he did, then he would have lied. Lying was very unoriginal. It would be far less commonplace to actually have told the truth.

So, the toaster must stay.

As he watched the toaster, Josh wondered if everyone thought the way he did. Did they all contemplate the overused nature of communication? Probably. He dare not actually hope he was really different than everyone else.

He kept staring at the toaster. Something about it hanging from the ceiling intrigued him. If one was to use it in the position, they could lay under it, and when the bread popped out, it would fall directly into their mouth.

Fascinating.

Since he had recovered slightly from his dose of human interaction, Josh sat up.

A second later, the toaster vanished into thin air. Or possibly thick air, depending on the humidity. Anyway, it vanished, leaving nothing but a swinging cord and a wide-eyed young man staring at the space it had just been occupying.

3: Josh's Shopping Plan is Defeated by an Extravert Friend

> ORIGINALITY.
> WHAT AN OVERRATED FALLACY.
> LOOKING AT TOASTERS IS MORE FUN.
> INFORM ME WHEN YOU TOO HAVE BEGUN.

Maria Higgins was staring at a toaster. This in itself was not particularly odd. Many people stare at toasters, and jump when the bread pops out. However, this toaster did not appear to have any bread in it, which was odd. That was perhaps the most odd thing, actually.

There were a few other slightly odd things about that particular toaster, though.

It was floating.[3]

Yes, Maria was staring at a floating toaster.

Her first thought, however, wasn't, *how in the world is that thing floating?* Her first thought was, *that's wired; toasters aren't alive.* Which was, of course, a perfectly logical thing to think.

Perhaps you would like to know why the toaster was floating. Well, explaining the physics of it is beyond modern science, or at least my knowledge of modern science, so I'm afraid I can't help you. The main thing you need to remember is that the toaster is, in fact, floating, and both it, and Maria, along a bunch of other living things, are, in fact, in the Cyber Void.

Oh, right, I didn't mention that. Well, they are. That's why Maria wasn't surprised to see the toaster floating. Everything in the Cyber Void sort of floated. At least, there seemed to be a sense of up and down, but there was nothing to stand on and no walls, no ceiling, and no ceiling fans.

Maria's real surprise came from the fact that the toaster was there at all. Up until that moment, everyone in the Cyber Void had believed only living things could be trapped there. But toasters were most definitely not alive...or at least they never had been to Maria's knowledge. Yet, here was one right in front of her, in the Cyber Void.

------

[3] On second thought, this might actually be more weird than its lack of bread.

Josh was avoiding it. He knew he was, and he also knew sooner or later he would have to do it.

Grocery shopping.

He hated it. Actually, there was nothing he particularly hated about *grocery* shopping, he just hated all shopping. It was boring, he had to interact with people, and it was so unoriginal. He had tried to make it an original experience, but as usual, he failed. So, today he decide to just get it over with as quickly as possible and not worry about trying to make it interesting.

He did have a few tactics to avoid getting into an uninteresting conversation. He would not look anyone in the eye, would walk very quickly, and always look very busy. His tactics usually worked pretty well, and his interactions would be limited to the cashier. His plan would have worked great this time too, if he had not literally run into someone on his way into the grocery store.

"Hey, Josh! Nice to see you out and about. You should really look where you are going though—you just about ran me over."

Brandon. Great. Josh muttered, "Sorry," and tried to sidestep him and escape inside the store.

"You should be! Just kidding. I'm glad you ran into me, otherwise we might have walked right past each other. By the way, the hike was awesome! You really missed out."

Josh paused, remembering something. He looked up at his friend. "Actually, after you left for your hike, something really strange happened. I've been meaning to tell you about it."

"Wow. I think that's the most words you have ever used in one sentence." Brandon grinned.

Josh rolled his eyes. "Unlikely."

"It must be really strange, if *you* think it is. Because what you think is normal is usually pretty weird. Can't wait to hear about it. Let's teleport over to that sandwich place for lunch."

"I was about to go shopping…"

"Too bad! You can do it later. And since when did you ever *want* to go shopping?"

"Fine, but I want to walk. Everyone uses the teleporters."

"No, Josh." Brandon looked him directly in the eye. "You are actually wrong. Not everyone uses them, and if you think about what mankind has done throughout history, walking is probably the most common, boring, overused form of getting somewhere."

"Wow, Brandon! That is probably the most logical sentence I have ever heard you say."

"Don't mention it, bro."

"The teleporter it is, then." Even Josh couldn't argue with that kind of logic. "Though it still isn't original."

Brandon laughed and patted his shoulder, which annoyed him very much. "Josh, being original is like running into a forty foot turquoise snail while thinking about quantum mechanics and reading the ingredients on a shampoo bottle—it doesn't happen."

"Your fatalistic mood is hardly commendable."

"I'm not being fatalistic," Brandin said, "I just didn't particularly care whether originality exists anymore. And, I think you'd have a lot more fun if you forgot this ridiculous

15

quest for the untried. Not that you ever are out to have fun—I think you like being miserable."[4]

Josh firmly decided not to grace his friend's statement with a reply. Not that replying really would have graced it. More likely, Josh's reply would have simply encouraged more unoriginal statements from his friend. Brandon was so normal.

Brandon motioned toward a blue box-like thing in front of the store. "Well, let's go, there's a telestation right over there."

Josh followed his friend over to the telestation and into the telebooth. He vaguely remembered something about teleportation had always made him uncomfortable...of course, it was considered perfectly safe, but the science of it bothered him. Something about how the person's consciousness was transferred from one place to another.

He then remembered he wasn't the only one. Many people had been uncomfortable with the use of teleporters. So, of course, it would be very illogical to be uncomfortable himself. He should just let all them be uncomfortable for him while he tried to figure out whether anyone had ever thought up Brandon's scenario with the giant snail before. Brandon, of all people, to come up with a statement that at least *sounded* original. Who would have guessed? Someone would have, though, of course.

Frustrated, but not really disturbed, Josh watched his friend type in the address of the sandwich place. He then activated the teleporter, and Josh waited to rematerialize in front of the restaurant.

---

[4] Josh did not like being miserable.

Josh did not rematerialize in front of the sandwich restaurant—or at least, not the same Josh who had walked into the telebooth. But then, are you really surprised? Nothing can ever go according to plan, not even things like teleportation.

After all, in a universe with disappearing toasters and said toasters floating in Cyber Voids, you really shouldn't expect anything to be normal. Or maybe you should, because it might be more interesting for you if you're constantly being surprised.

Anyway, let's just say that Josh and Brandon regretted using that teleporter—and regretted every other time they had ever used a teleporter in their entire lives.

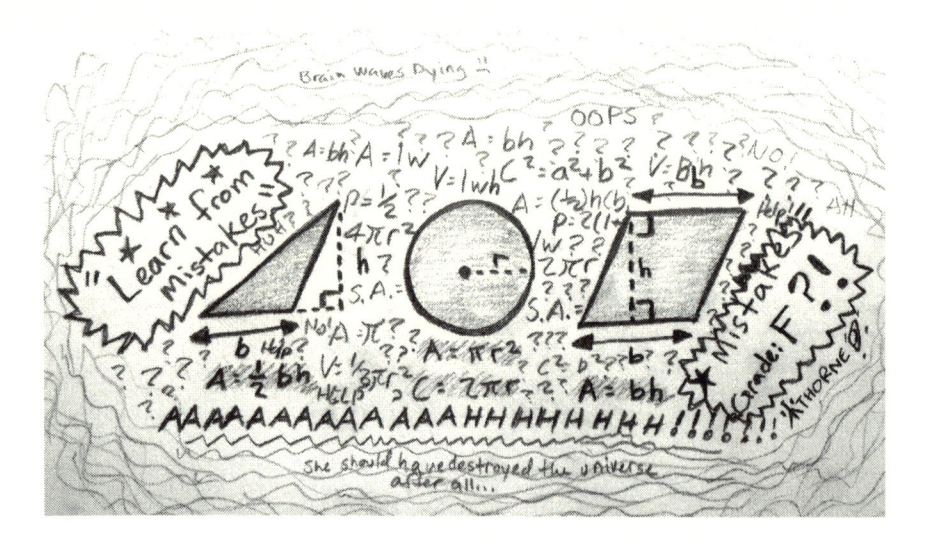

4: Learning From Mistakes Gone Wrong

> YES, I MADE A MISTAKE.
> YES, I ATE YOUR CAKE.
> I HOPE YOU CAN FORGIVE ME,
> BEFORE I DRINK YOUR TEA.

Someone had once told Rachel Mew she could learn from her mistakes. That someone was her geometry teacher, Robert Knot. He had obviously learned a lot, so Rachel listened to him.

She decided, as she hadn't been able to learn anything the way she was doing it, she'd start learning from mistakes. It seemed like a brilliant new idea. Rachel made as many mistakes as she could, thinking that no doubt her next geometry test would be perfect. Learn from your mistakes, right? If you learn from mistakes, shouldn't you make as many as possible?

Needless to say, Rachel Mew did learn from her mistakes—just not exactly in the way she'd been hoping. She learned there was a difference between geometry teachers and most other people: they said confusing things that didn't work in real life. Mr. Knot apologized and let her retake the test, and Rachel could tell he thought her rather amusing—and felt sorry for her.

Rachel also learned from her mistake that learning from mistakes didn't exactly work for her. (And she didn't see a bit of contradiction in that thought, no matter what Maria said.)

This whole episode had been the only time she and the geometry teacher really had anything to do with each other, so of course you can forgive her for not knowing he was actually the most brilliant scientist of all time—or at least, of all the time that anyone could think of or know about.

You can also forgive her for thinking he was human. You may wonder why you have to forgive her for this, but I will explain. Your misconception lies in imagining Robert Knot is human. Because, he isn't.

He is actually of the species *Aleo slieneos*, known by the common name alien. He came from the planet mud. Mud is very much like earth. It's the same color, same texture, and the same size. Hence, there has been much confusion as to whether the two are, in fact, different things. Many people use the two words interchangeably. But, this is very incorrect, as Robert Knot would attest. Earth is inhabited by humans, mud by aliens. Earth is orbited by the moon, mud by the satellite. Earth orbits the sun, mud orbits the star. The people are different too. Earthlings are obsessed with power, greed, and selfishness. Mudlings are obsessed with—well, even Robert had to admit they lived for basically the same things.

There was just one striking difference between the two worlds and two races.

Aliens were the first to visit an extrastellar planet.

Well, *visit* is a bit of a stretch. It was actually a complete mistake. Robert Knot got the coordinates of his micro-wormhole-transporter a bit wrong. So, voywolla! There he was, on earth. Don't tell me voywolla isn't really a word, because I know that, and I don't really care. It perfectly expresses the reaction of Robert Knot.

Anyway though, it was a mistake, and that was the lightbulb moment in Robert's life when he realized one could, really, learn from their mistakes. Yes, they could learn never to put the wrong coordinates into the transporter. And to not use anything remotely akin to the transporter to begin with.

The earthlings' teleporting machine was very much like his wormhole-transporter on mud, so he hadn't used it.

Except for an experiment. He was curious how many random objects he could teleport out of people's homes before someone figured out what he was doing.

It was a very useful experiment—almost as useful as the study he had been doing before he left mud. He'd been studying whether killing oneself was logical because of how it protected you from dying in the future. He then proposed that everyone who was afraid of dying should kill themselves right away, and their fear would instantly vanish, never to return again. For some unexplained reason, his results were never published in mud's scientific magazines.

So, the alien of the planet mud was teleporting random objects to his office in his spare time after the geometry class.

He was doing this when Josh's toaster disappeared. He was also doing this then two other toasters disappeared, both of them belonging to, of all people, his former student Rachel Mew.

And when Miss Mew's two kitchen appliances[5] disappeared, she teleported right over to the police station to report it.

But she never got to the police station—of course.

---

[5] Meaning the toasters, of course.

This page is intentionally left blank.

Blank, did you say? I'm sorry, but that page is most definitely not blank. It clearly has writing on it. Or, do you mean blank in the sense of "lacking" as in "My question was met with a *blank* stare"? But then, I can hardly see why you would intentionally leave an entire page of your book like that.

An entire page! How could you? What a waste! Do you have any idea how many trees had to be killed to create that page, which you are wasting by leaving it blank? Or very nearly blank. Oh, you really don't see any contradiction about writing that a page is blank on the very page you are saying is blank? Or maybe it is just a conundrum. Maybe there is some possible way the page can be blank and have writing on it at the same time. Nonsense! What has the human race come to?

The alien race at least admits that to have no absolute truth, there must be absolute truth, and to say all morality is relative, it must be relative to something non-relative. Or they do some of the time. Ugh. Can't anything be simple anymore? But that is assuming at some point things were simple, which is probably not true.

In a universe where blank pages have writing on them, one must be careful not to forget the storyline by running down rabbit trails. Speaking of which, what were the characters doing? Oh, that's right, they all went to Mars. Mars? No! Mars isn't cool enough anymore. They actually went to Undkeldmejfxx. Or something with a name like that. Because, in fantasy and sci-fi, the best judge of a good story is how unpronounceable the names are. Seriously. What are you saying? They went to the planet mud! Of all the boring, dull, uninspiring names! I wonder who thought of it. As if anyone would read a book with a planet called mud. Why, that's almost as bad as calling a planet earth! Wait, they've *done* that? Wow, I feel sorry for those people. That's almost as bad calling your solar system the "solar system" or your moon the "moon." Oh, they've done that too? Where are these people's imaginations? No wonder they invented fiction!

But you're wrong about them going to mud, anyway, because Robert Knot hasn't gone anywhere except earth and his office, and nobody else has gone anywhere except the Cyber Void.

5: Revisiting the Floating Toaster

> WRITING TIPS 101: WHEN YOU DON'T KNOW WHAT TO WRITE, WRITE A BLOG POST ABOUT IT.

In case you haven't realized, the Cyber Void is going to have a lot to do with this story. So, maybe it's time you find out what the Cyber Void actually is. Maybe. Well, fine. I will explain.

The Cyber Void exists because of one thing only: the main teleportation operating system. This system prefers to be referred to as a "she." And, her name is Telena.

Telena is the cyber intelligence controlling all the individual telestations. Whenever a new person is put in the Cyber Void, she gives a short, prerecorded, explanation for them, to let them know why they are there. For some reason,

25

she thinks knowing they are stranded in an empty void, for, well, *forever*, will be comforting to them. Or maybe, she doesn't think about it at all. She is just a computer program. In fact, she is kind of a broken computer program.[6]

Anyway, this is what she tells them:

"Welcome to the Cyber Void. You are here because you used the teleporter and a copy of you was sent to a new location. That left me with the original you: your mind and body. My programming instructed me to void your body at the same moment your new copy appeared in the specified location. So, that is what I have done with your body. But my programming gave no instructions on what to do with your mind. So, I have created the Cyber Void: a virtual place for your mind to exist after your body has been destroyed. You will now live on here virtually forever."

Maria, Josh, Brandon, and Rachel all heard this message when they found themselves suspended in the Cyber Void.

Oh, yes, they were all in the Cyber Void. They were not all together, however. Rachel and Maria didn't know they were both there. Josh and Brandon did know they were both there, but were intentionally not together.

Brandon had found several previous copies of himself and was enjoying talking to them immensely. They had a lot in common with each other. And by that, I mean they had everything in common with each other up until the moment each of them entered the Void.

Josh, on the other hand, was not enjoying anything and was bemoaning the fact that he ever knew Brandon. Brandon

---

[6] Or perhaps, the people who created her program are the ones who are really broken. Food for thought.

had convinced him to use the teleporter in the first place! Josh would have been happy (if Josh could ever really be called happy) walking. Now, Josh could not even walk if he wanted to. All he could do was kind of...float around. So, he'd decide to float away from Brandon and see if he could find anything interesting. Brandon—or should I say *Brandons*—were definitely not interesting at the moment.

It didn't take Josh long to come to the conclusion the Cyber Void was the last place he would have ever wanted to be in. Nothing, absolutely *nothing*, original ever happened. (At least, it hadn't during the brief period of time he'd spent there already.)

He thought his life had been boring before, but now he was starting to realize just how original it had been. Living in the Cyber Void, he could only do two things: talk to himself, or talk to someone else.

Talking to himself could mean two different things: actually talking to him, or talking to a previous version of him. They, all of the Joshes that he had met stuck in the Void, did not like talking, so talking to himself was no more interesting than it had ever been before. And let's be honest—it had never been *very* interesting.

But, things were about to change for Josh. No, he was not going to start finding it interesting to talk to himself, or previous versions of himself. Actually, he was about to get hit in the head by a floating toaster. *His* floating toaster. The same toaster that disappeared from his room.

Maria Higgins was still staring at a toaster. This toaster was the most interesting thing she'd seen in a long time. Suddenly, it floated right into the head of a man who was floating nearby. He jumped—as well as one could jump when already floating. She guessed he was not in the habit of looking out for floating objects, and especially toasters. But really, is anyone actually in the habit of looking out for floating toasters?

He was still looking at it with astonishment when he blurted out, "That's my toaster!"

"What?"

"It's my toaster! I had it hanging above my bed and then it just disappeared."

Maria raised her eyebrows. "You had a toaster hanging above your bed?"

"Yes, I was trying to be original. Anyway, how did it get here?"

"I don't know. It just appeared like all the people do. Who are you, anyway? I don't think I've met you or any version of you before. What's your name?"

"Josh."

"Ok. So, your toaster doesn't happen to be alive, right? Because, it really shouldn't be here. Only living things are stored in the Cyber Void. Except, of course, for our clothes and anything else we were wearing when we teleported." A thought occurred to her. "Wait," she exclaimed, "don't tell me you were somehow *wearing* the toaster when you teleported!"

"No, of course it's not alive. And I wasn't wearing it. It's just an average, boring, toaster. The sad thing is, when I hung it from the ceiling, I really thought I had finally thought of something new and original! Then, I found out someone had already done it. I wonder if anyone has ever worn a toaster before, though..."

Maria found herself staring, not at the toaster, but at Josh. The toaster was still floating near his head, and every now and then it bumped into him. He didn't look extraordinary; just kind of comical. But, he had thought to hang a toaster from his ceiling. Now, *that* was impressive! She'd certainly never thought of doing that.

"So..." she said, "if it was hanging above your bed, did you ever try toasting bread in it from that position?"

"No, I was just thinking about that when it disappeared."

"The bread would fall right into your mouth."

"Yes! That is the same thing I was thinking when it disappeared!"

"Really? That's crazy, though! The bread would hit you in the face and burn you. It would put crumbs in your bed. That would be like sleeping with sand in your bed. Gross! Who eats bread in their bed anyway?"

"You're right, it's pretty stupid."

"No, I think it's great! If I ever get out of here, I want to try it."

Josh and Maria both stopped talking and just stared at each other. Neither of them could believe what they'd just been doing.

Josh was ruining everything he'd worked so hard on. He was talking to someone using boring, overused, words and saying nothing original. Part of him felt exceedingly annoyed with himself, but oddly, the other part of him really did not

29

care at all. He started to wonder whether all the time he'd spent trying to be original had been worth it. What difference did it really make if he was original or not? Now that he was stuck in the Cyber Void, being original just didn't seem quite as important.

As for Maria, she was annoyed because of Josh. Not that she found Josh annoying—no, it was the fact that she liked him that annoyed her. She had tried for so long to erase all thoughts of romance from her mind. Of course, she hadn't been entirely successful, but she had tried very hard. Now, this strange guy who hung a toaster above his bed was starting to make her waver in her resolve.

Maria was also having a philosophical and grammatical debate with herself as to whether liking someone was the same as *liking* someone and having a boy friend was the same as having a *boyfriend*, and if Josh became her friend, which category he would fit into, and whether she wanted to risk being around him if he fit into the wrong one. Ugh.

Suddenly, they both realized they were staring at each other. They looked away quickly, trying to pretend they'd been looking at something else.[7]

"So," said Maria, trying to brake the awkward silence. And it had been awkward. Not because silence is always awkward, because sometimes talking can be more awkward than silence. Like, if you are in church, braking the silence could definitely be a lot more awkward for you and for everyone else. But, this silence was awkward, so Maria

---

[7] This was difficult, considering the lack of other things to look at in the Cyber Void.

decided talking and braking the silence was the less awkward of the two options.

Josh was about to say something when the toaster floated in between them again. He gave it a shove and it floated off.

"Seriously! What is it with the toasters?" he said, shaking his head.

"I know! Really, there is nothing interesting about them! They just toast bread. They sit around most of the time doing nothing. Just a boring kitchen appliance."

"And yet we are both still talking about them!"

"Well, it is the most interesting thing I've seen in a while. A floating toaster! And then you showed up and it hits you in the head and you just stand there like you're in shock— probably because you are."

"But it's *my* toaster! Don't you think that's a bit odd? I wasn't even teleporting it. It just disappeared out of my bedroom by itself."

"Someone must have teleported it. But it still shouldn't be here! It's not alive."

"Well..." said Josh, and the silence became awkward again.

31

THE Brandons

6: Rachel Becomes an Honorary Member of the Bro Manly-Man Club

> WRITING TIPS 101: TO BE A NOVELIST, YOU DON'T HAVE TO ACTUALLY WRITE A NOVEL. YOU JUST HAVE TO CONVINCE EVERYONE ELSE THAT YOU KNOW HOW TO WRITE ONE, AND THEN WRITE ABOUT THAT.

One, two, three, four...twenty...

Someone had used the teleporter a lot. Rachel found out who he was rather quickly, as a great crowd of him had gathered together to talk. She found herself staring at him (or them) for quite some time.

He was kind of loud and careless seeming, joking with all the versions of himself and updating them on the latest outside the Void news. They liked to call this news *The Voidette*.

His later versions were around Rachel's age—well, a little older—with shaggy blond hair and bright, like *really* bright, bluish green eyes. He was average height and kind of broad. Not overweight though, Rachel noticed with regret. Not that she really wanted other people to be like her, but seeing people of the correct weight made her remember her own shortcomings—or widecomings, depending on how she thought about it.

His name was Brandon, and she knew this because the different versions of him seemed to enjoy calling each other by name in just about every sentence.

"Hey Brandon, you need to cut your hair," said a Brandon —he appeared around fifteen.

"I was going to," replied the other Brandon, who looked older. "It keeps falling into my face." He ran his fingers back through it until it all stuck up on end, and Rachel almost laughed. It wasn't really that long, but extremely messy.

"Hey Brandon," said a younger Brandon, maybe around ten. "Did we ever beat that old Kevin guy who thought he was the arm wrestling champion?"

"Yup Brandon, sure did. A few months ago. You all shoulda seen his face. And you should have heard Josh when I told him. 'That was hardly unexpected.' There's nothing you can do to surprise that kid!"

"Oh, Josh would just love to hear us calling him a kid."

"Actually, he wouldn't care."

"I know."

"Yeah."

"So you beat old Kevin, Brandon? Well, we are strong. Always thought so."

"Yeah Brandon, we're pretty awesome."

"Sure are."

Rachel wasn't sure whether she wanted to gag or laugh. Most people's copies, including her own, avoided each other. Not the Brandons! Such a ridiculous group of guys, all enjoying their time together, by themselves—and quite literally themselves.

No one else was hanging out—and "hanging" was definitely the right word—listening to the Brandons' conversation. She supposed most people considered them, at the very least, extremely odd, and had avoided sticking around.

Finally, someone noticed her.

"Oh, hi," one of the Brandons said to Rachel, and shook her hand.

"Hi."

Another one of them chimed in. "I've met you—or one of you—before. Rachel Higgins, isn't it? Your favorite movie was *Arrogance and Bias*."

"Yes, it was my favorite a year ago. But you haven't met me. I just got here a little bit ago."

"Oh, so did I," said the Brandon who had said "hi" to her. "I haven't met you. Or, I hadn't until just now."

"Do you all have...numbers...or something?" Rachel asked, looking around at the mostly identical group of people.

"No, just name."

"It's confusing."

One of them grinned, throwing his arm around another's shoulders. "It's awesome."

"You really enjoy seeing so many literal copies of yourself?"

"You don't?"

"No, I really don't. It makes me sick. Seeing myself in a mirror is bad enough."

"Really? I like mirrors," said a different Brandon.

"No, I don't. Don't be stupid, Brandon," said the "hi" Brandon. Rachel decided she was going to call him that from then on. He would be Hi Brandon. Hi would be like his name. Hi Brandon was wearing a tan t-shirt and blue jeans, and had a black watch. That was how she'd tell him apart. The rest of them on the other hand...

"So, *Arrogance and Bias* a year ago. Never watched it. What do you like now?"

Rachel Mew didn't exactly want to tell him. She knew it wasn't cool. It was all Maria's fault for getting her to watch it. "*Star Hike*—the first old series."

"Really? That's ancient. They've rebooted it thirty-eight times since then—almost as much as *Star Fights*."

"Oh, I like *Star Fights* too."

"Really? You've got to meet Josh, because seriously, that's original! Liking *Star Hike* and *Star Fights*, both, together, simultaneously—that's almost as uncommon as my thing with the forty-foot snail. And being a girl too—no offense. And a girl who also likes *Arrogance and Bias*. And liking the OLD *Star Hikes* too, where the rocks look like cardboard. Wow!"

35

Rachel had never been called original, and doubted she really was. And if she was, it was all because of Maria, because she would have probably been watching soap operas without her friend. Instead, she was watching ancient outdated space westerns... Okay, it was still an improvement.

"So," Hi Brandon announced, "I think we have a new honorary member to the Bro Manly-Man Club. Please welcome, Rachel Mew!"

Cheers erupted from the group of Brandons. Bro manly-man cheers.

Rachel blushed, which turned her face splotchy red, and wasn't at all attractive. "But I am a girl," she said.

Hi Brandon clapped her on the shoulder. "That's why you're an *honorary* member. Also, we had literally just made up the club name before you floated over here. We were seriously sick of being called the Brandon Bunch."

"Well, thanks, I guess," Rachel said. She laughed. "If I ever form a Sis Womanly-Woman Club, I'll be sure to include you."

Brandon bowed. "I would be honored."

Rachel giggled and blushed again. Her heart had started to flutter and she found herself looking anywhere except Hi Brandon's ridiculously green eyes.

Oh, she thought. *Oh, no.*

7: The Problem With Environmentally Friendly Buildings

> IT'S THE SPEED LIMIT.
> IT'S NOT A SUGGESTION.
> SO, PLEASE SLOW DOWN—
> DON'T HIT THE PEDESTRIANS!

When a policemen showed up on Robert Knot's doorstep, the esteemed math teacher was surprised. He'd only been able to teleport three toasters before being caught.

"Mr. Knot," said the policeman, giving him a highly disappointed and disapproving look of disappointed disapproval.

This look struck instant guilt into Knot's guilty soul, and he held up his hands. "Yes, yes. I'll admit it—it's me. I'm the one who's been teleporting the toasters. I only got to teleport three of them, so bravo on the police work. Bravo! I can explain, though, I promise. I was doing an experiment, you see..." He frowned, as the disappointment and disapproval on the policeman's face was replaced with befuddled confusion.

"What?" the poor fellow said. "I'm not sure I completely understand anything you just told me. Although, now I'm thinking about it, there was a young lady named Rachel who reported missing her toasters. I thought it was a little odd how she said *toasters*, because I'm not really sure why anyone needs more than one, but maybe she has a big family or something."

"Or maybe she just liked toasters," Knot mused. "I kind of like them myself, though I never toast bread. Toasters just look good on the counter, if you know what I mean. I never can understand why on earth people toast bread in the first place, though! Back on mud, we stopped that barbaric practice a long time ago. You see, burnt bread was one of the leading causes of cancer back home, so it just kind of lost popularity with people."

The policeman nodded, scratching his stubbly chin with one hand. "Well, I don't toast much bread myself anymore. Used to toast a couple pieces every morning, but I got tired of waiting for it to finish, so I started buying that pre-toasted stuff. No quite as good, but it does save me a few minutes. I still have the old toaster, though. Never could bring myself to part with it."

Robert Knot gave a thoughtful nod, then frowned slightly. "Why exactly are you here, though? It's fine with me if you just wanted to talk about your toasting, but back home police didn't do that sort of thing, at least not any I ever heard of. Maybe it's different on earth. It is usually the little differences that surprise me the most. You did come here because of my experiment, right?"

"No, I don't know a thing about your experiment. But if it has anything to do with stealing toasters, you'd better stop."

Knot's face lit up in a toothy grin. "Oh, this is great! I mean it. Truly great! I've made another mistake. I thought for sure you came about the experiment, and now I've told you all about it."

"Yeah, well, I don't see anything good about it for you. I mean, you've just turned yourself in to me."

Robert waved his hand. "No, no, you wouldn't. But it *is* great for me because now I can learn from it. Ever since I made the mistake of coming here, I've learned to learn from all my mistakes."

By this point, the policeman had forgotten why he'd been knocking on Mr. Knot's door to begin with. Something to do with laws about how hard teachers were allowed to make math problems. Ah, that was it!

He straightened abruptly. "Mr. Robert Knot, this is you first and final warning. You are NOT to give your students problems that make them feel foolish."

"What on mud are you talking about?" exclaimed Robert, who had still not gotten entirely into the habit of remembering he was on earth. It did take a lot of remembering, too, though he was not exactly sure why.

39

The policeman gave his voice a threatening growl. "Just today, two students reported to me that you gave them problems which were above their *very high* skill level."

Knot's eyebrows shot up. He hadn't given a semi-challenging problem in months. "What students?"

"I'm sorry. Student-police confidentiality."

"Now wait just a minute! Were they Jimmy Jimm Jim and Wilma Wilson?"

The policeman's face gave it away.

Robert tossed up his hands. "Those are literally the stupidest children in my class! If I bring everything down to their level, no one will learn anything."

"Oh, don't be *daft*. We all know children learn best when they can relate to their peers on the same level. You must teach to the lowest student or their self-esteem will be hurt and they will feel left behind by their friends."

"Daft yourself! They *should* be left behind!"

"How could you? They are just as special as the other students and deserve you to teach at their level."

"Just like they deserve participation trophies at every contest? Seriously, at least on mud we knew when we had lost!"[8]

"Sir, I would be careful," admonished the policeman.

"Careful? Your education system is ridiculous! Absolutely ridiculous. If I can't teach children what two plus two is, what are they going to do when they need to find the area of a circle? I mean, you've outlawed the use of pi because it gave

---

[8] The difference was, on mud, they made losing just as great as winning, so no one would feel worse than anyone else, anyway.

a student a headache, and you outlawed exponents too, almost."

The policeman shrugged. "I don't know about most of what you said, but as far as I know, we haven't outlawed pie. I just ate some the other night, in fact. I can't imagine why you would think it's been outlawed. It's really a great dessert. Love it! I'm sorry about the student who got the headache. Maybe they were allergic to one of the ingredients, say nuts, or eggs."

"Sir, you prove my point exactly," said Knot, backing up a few paces as if the policeman was frightening in his misunderstandings. Which indeed he was, as few things are more frightening than grown men who don't know math. After all, one of them might get in control of the country one day, and horrible things could happen. Like, if they thought they were cutting taxes and actually doubled them. Yikes! That would be almost as bad as extraterrestrials invading, and much less interesting.

"Mr. Knot, I think you really ought to be careful," the policeman said again.

"Careful of what?" Robert cried. "Nuts and eggs in pi. Now that's weird—really, it's strange. A diameter of six point five centimeters multiplied by pi, which is three point fourteen if you round it, now multiply that by nuts and then by eggs. Maybe that's part of the problem with schools nowadays. They're run by nuts. They multiply the nuts, and then the nuts become rotten eggs. And then they stink. Yes, maybe that's the problem with schools."

The policeman stared at him. "Mr. Robert Knot, you are completely insane."

41

"No, I'm Knot."

"I say you are."

"No, I say I am. I've been Knot—Robert Knot—since, oh, I don't know."

"You sir, had better be careful. Insurance doesn't cover this kind of stuff anymore."

"What, are you threatening me?"

"No, I'm just warning you." The policeman said, his eyes becoming rounder by the second.

"What in the world is wrong?" Robert replied, taking another step back. The policeman blanched.

"Seriously," Robert went on. "You're dreadfully frightened. I wonder... I was doing a sort of study back on mud. About suicide. You know, how if you're afraid of death, doing it might make sense. It even protects you from things like stubbing your toe. I haven't tried this remedy, though. You see, I'm not really afraid of death. I mean, I've never died before, so why would I worry about it happening in the future? That's just worry-phobia. Or something."

"Please stop," the police begged. "I've dealt with suicide cases before, but never with delusional people like you. So can you please just—"

Robert Knot took another step back, and his foot came down on air. The poor policeman stifled a scream.

It now becomes relevant to understand one small fact about geometry teacher Robert Knot's humble abode: it happened to be eighteen stories up on a skyscraper. And he'd just fallen off of his porch.

No, perhaps the building design wasn't the safest, but it was environmentally friendly, so no one really cared.

Anyway, Robert had just fallen from great heights. (Actually, he was still falling.)

The policeman clung to the bit of railing on the stairs. (Yes, there was railing on the stairs, but not on the porch.) "Well, this is really bad," he mumbled to himself. "He's got to be toast. No one would survive a fall like that. What am I going to do? This is really very terrible! Very bad! I just can't stand the thought of it. That poor man! And he was such a nice sort of fellow even if he did talk funny sometimes."

8: Buying Mattresses From the Moon

> **WRITING WISDOM 101:** IF YOU'VE BEEN WORKING ON ONE BOOK FOR A MULTITUDE OF YEARS, CHANCES ARE...YOU HAVEN'T ACTUALLY BEEN WORKING ON IT.

Falling from eighteen stories up is an experience that usually has fatal consequences. So, you can forgive the policeman for thinking Robert Knot was toast.

Before you start worrying too much about the policeman's mental state, he did not actually believe Robert turned into a piece of toasted bread when he fell; he was just using an expression. However, to tell the truth, his mental state really was not the greatest. And unfortunately for him, it was about to get a lot worse.

But not for Robert.

Unless Mr. Knot had been trying to kill himself (which he had not been), things were about to get better for him.

"As I was saying," Robert shouted up from the street below, as he lay flat on his back on the pavement. "Committing suicide is something to look into if you're afraid of dying. I really was not trying to kill myself just now; I just forgot about the porch not having railings. We used to have railings on the porches back home, but not on the stairs! It always is the little things that get me—like my toe! It hurts like crazy! I think I must have stubbed it when I fell."

"You're not dead?" the policeman stuttered.

The wind must have been blowing just right, or perhaps Mr. Knot had extraordinary ears, because he heard the policeman perfectly. "No!" he shouted back, still lying there. "I am completely dead. As dead as you get. Sorry, I just seem to have fallen into a sar-chasm of sorts. Anyway though, no, really, I'm not dead in the least. I've never felt better. Except for my toe. It hurts like crazy. I should probably go put some ice on it."

Robert promptly stood up, and started climbing the stairs to his house. The policeman also stood up, but this was a very bad idea for him. Like I said, his mental state was bad enough when Robert fell. And although it would seem like it should have improved when he found out Mr. Knot didn't suffer any fatal consequences from his fall,[9] it actually worsened significantly.

When Robert reached his porch, the policeman backed away from him as if he were a ghost. This is quite possibly

---

[9] A stubbed toe does not count as a fatal consequence, even if Robert would have liked to disagree.

45

because he thought Robert was a ghost, but we will *not* forgive him for this, because it was clear Robert was *not* a ghost...or at least, it should have been clear to any rationally-minded person. But then again, the policemen never had been a very rationally minded person.

"Hey, you should really be careful!" Robert said, as the policeman continued to back away from him, and ever closer to the edge of the porch.

"You're not dead!" The policeman took a few hurried steps back. Humans have an odd habit of stating the obvious sometimes, and the policeman was engaging in this habit. "You're really not dead!"

"Are you sure? You don't sound very sure. Maybe—hey, really! You're going to fall off!"

The policeman, completely oblivious to Robert's words, walked right off of the porch and plummeted to the street below.

"This is terrible!" Knot said. "He's got to be dead. And he was such a nice fellow, even if he was a little daft about math."

Now, you may be wondering why Robert is worried about him at all, since he just made the same fall with few real consequences. You see, however, Knot was a rational thinker. He knew, even though he wasn't sure yet why he'd survived, that it was unlikely the law of gravity had changed. Therefore, a person should still die from falling eighteen stories.[10]

He also made the rational choice to go put ice on his toe before going down to see what had become of the poor

---

[10] Eighteen stories is roughly one hundred and eighty feet.

policeman. You may think him terribly insensitive for not running down right away, but here you would be wrong. Knot figured—and he is a math teacher, so it is only natural he should think in figures—that if the policeman had survived the fall in the same way he had, he would probably be perfectly fine. Or, at least, would only have minor injuries, like a stubbed toe or a scraped knee.

And if he had died, well, there was nothing Mr. Knot could do about it anyway.

<hr />

The couple who lived on the street level eighteen stories below Robert's house had a habit of making poor decisions. They didn't make poor decisions because they were poor—many poor people make good decisions—but they were poor because they made poor decisions.

And, they made a lot of them. Their first poor decision involved chewing gum and silly putty, but this decision has zero relevance here, except as being their first poor decision. Therefore, we will not elaborate on it any further.

At that moment, they were making the poor decision to buy eighty-five thousand dollar king-sized mattresses. Yes, plural. They were actually buying five of them. No one really knew why, especially since their current fifty-five thousand dollar mattresses were in nearly perfect condition.

Worse than their poor decision about buying the mattresses to begin with, they had gotten them on a loan. The loan had a one hundred and fifty year payment plan... but that is also irrelevant.

They were getting their new mattresses installed, and had just laid them all out in front of their apartment. Yes, they laid them all out, all five of them, in the time between when Robert fell and when the policeman fell. This fact goes to show they had no good excuse for being poor when they could be such remarkably fast workers when they wanted to be.

The five mattresses took up so much room they almost blocked off the entire street. And then, it happened. The unthinkable, the unimaginable happened. One of the mattresses was half a centimeter larger than the others. It was horrifying! A major flaw! That mattress would be worth thousands of dollars less now! But, of course, they didn't want a flawed mattress. No! They would send it back and get it replaced by a perfectly-sized new one.

While the purchasers were arguing this over the phone with the manufacturer, a rather unnoticeable thing happened.

A man fell onto one of the mattresses.

Not a single person noticed. Just a man falling from eighteen stories up and landing smack dab in the center of a massive mattress surrounded by four more massive mattresses all laid out in front of an apartment on the street.

It was unnoticeable because no one noticed and it was unremarkable because no one remarked on it. Not that they wouldn't have if they had seen it happen, but they had simply not been looking.

Robert's hypothesis was correct. The policeman suffered only very minor injuries from the fall. In fact, the only real consequence was that he did not remember anything he'd done since he started walking down the street towards Robert's house.

So, he rolled off the mattress and stood up, scratched his head, and tried to remember why he had walked down this particular street in the first place.

In the meantime, the mattresses' purchasers were still on the phone with the manufacturer. They'd come to a most satisfactory agreement. The manufacturer said, if they would ship the oversized mattress back, they could buy a new one, and this time they would guarantee it was the correct size. Shipping could be a little high though—in more ways than one. The mattresses happened to be manufactured on the moon.

The policeman, running his fingers though his hair a few more times and sticking his hands deep into his pants pockets, finally landed on why he must have been walking down the street. He had actually quite literally landed on it a few moments ago. The mattresses! They were almost completely blocking off the street. A definite traffic violation.

Thus, he immediately started the intense job of policing everyone. The end result was that he never remembered about how Robert Knot had not died. In fact, no one remembered this one important fact except Robert himself, who was having a dreadfully complicated argument with himself about whether or not reality was real anymore and whether the laws of physics still applied to him.

9: Josh Decides "HI" Might Be a Nice Thing to Say

> POETRY
> WAS GRACEFUL
> UNTIL I WROTE IT

Remember how Josh and Maria were talking in the Cyber Void? Or rather, remember how they weren't talking because of that terribly awkward silence? (And I don't blame you if you don't remember, because it's been awhile. So, don't think for a moment that I'm judging you for having an extremely short-term memory, and that I think a goldfish could do a better job remembering than you have. Because, that wouldn't be the case at all.)

Anyway...as it turned out, they never had to break the awkward silence because someone else did it for them.

Rachel.

She'd floated over from...somewhere...and, ever since she and Maria found each other, they had been talking nonstop. Currently, they were having a very animated discussion about a TV show called *Physician Whom*. Before being stuck in the Cyber Void, Maria had started watching this TV show. Now, she was trying to convince Rachel, who had not seen it yet (and probably never would now that she was in the Void) that it might actually be better that the old *Star Hikes*.

Having seen neither of the shows, Josh was forced to revert to his old habit of listening to the conversations of other people. He already wished he could flop on his bed. Actually, it didn't even have to be *his* bed. Any bed would do at this point.

People. Boring people.

When Josh met Maria, he felt like she might have been someone he could finely relate to; someone who understood him...at least a little tiny bit. He'd never had a best friend. Yes, he had Brandon, and Brandon had always tried to be a good friend, but Josh had never tried particularly hard to be a very good friend to Brandon.

Sure, he tolerated Brandon and would even admit that he enjoyed his company most of the time, but he just did not feel like he could relate to Brandon in any meaningful way. He found the conversations they had rather painfully boring, nor could he understand why Brandon kept on trying with him.

They were just so different. Brandon got along with everyone and loved talking, making Josh practically his exact opposite. The word Josh most often used to describe himself was *awkward*. He'd never valued human relationships very much, and would rather do things by himself. Of course, his obsession with originality and the overused nature of communication had not helped him make very many friends.

But the more Josh thought about his life, the more he realized he was, in fact, a very selfish person. He had not cared how his refusal to talk made Brandon feel. He'd never considered anyone else's feelings about anything he'd ever done. Okay, that might be a slight exaggeration, but you get the point. He spent and wasted his time feeling sorry for himself because he did not find life interesting.

But maybe, he'd never tried to find it interesting. Maybe, he'd always been looking for originality and interest in the wrong things. That was it! He'd always been looking for it in *things*, not *people*. (His toaster was a perfect example.)

He'd never tried to find people interesting. Ironically, they were now literally the only thing left for him to find interesting.[11]

He looked at Maria and Rachel. He could see nothing in common between the two of them. And yet, they appeared to be having a better time talking about an old TV show than Josh had had in his entire life.

He thought again about Brandon. He wished he'd gone on that hike with him. No, he probably would not have enjoyed it, but Brandon had wanted him to come. Once again, Josh had only been thinking about himself.

---

[11] Except that he did still have his toaster.

He wondered what his copy—what *he*—was doing outside of the void. He'd been going to eat lunch with Brandon. He wished he could tell the outside version of himself to live a little. When he saw Brandon next, or some version or versions of him, he would say "hi" and he didn't care if it had been said by basically every human that had ever lived hundreds of times throughout their lives. Maybe "hi" was just a nice thing to say.

10: Playing Toaster Volleyball in the Cyber Void

> I HAD A POEM HERE,
> BUT IT WAS STUPID,
> SO,
> I DELETED IT.

To the more intelligent members of society, it has long been clear that balls are not actually toys. They are, in fact, lingering and cruel objects used to support division between those who might otherwise have been friends.

It does not matter what kind of balls they are—soccer balls, baseballs, softballs, four-square balls, footballs, ping-pong balls, beach balls, golf balls, volleyballs—they all possess the same fatal flaw.

As I was saying, all the "innocent" round objects considered toys by the uneducated masses are truly ways to spit society.

Using a frightening psychological phenomenon known as athletic ability, balls divide people into one of two groups. Either they are Good With Balls or they are *Not* Good With Balls.

The humans who are Good With Balls enjoy them very much, as they enforce their animalistic feelings of superiority. Because clearly, being able to hit or kick an unnaturally round object in a repetitive and predictable manner has a great deal to do with being superior.

Well, but then the people who are *Not* Good With Balls have similar fantasies. They begin to think those who are Good With Balls were simply born that way without a bit of practice. Thus, they lead themselves to believe there is no point in trying to achieve the same unattainable, and rather useless, heights.

There have, of course, been efforts made to unite the divided athletic society, and include those *Not* Good With Balls as a part of the game.

Most of these efforts have epically failed.

I will elaborate on one of the ploys to end sports division. It is called the "team." Two people are chosen to be the "team leaders" and the rest are told to stand in a straight line. Then, taking turns, each of the "team leaders" pick people for their teams until no one is left in the line.

At first, this plan may seem brilliant. It divides the teams perfectly, and absolutely no one gets left out or gets their feelings get hurt. At least, not if they're chosen *first*.

However, it is actually an example of one of the most cruel forms of athletic injustice. Not only must the people chosen last endure the shame of knowing for themselves that they fit into the *Not* Good With Balls category, but they stand there while it is announced to the rest of the people in the game. And the lovely "team leaders" are allowed to judge them without any remorse.

Our friend, Rachel Mew, had always fit firmly into the category of *Not* Good With Balls. Even when she tried to find games involving balls fun or interesting, the fact that her skill levels were outside the ordinary made that hard. Outside the ordinary, in the sense that they were below the ordinary. It actually made her point zero, zero, zero—lots more zeros— one, percent *special*. And like the other things that made her special and different, it also made her unhappy.

Therefore, when Hi Brandon suggested they play a game called Toaster Volleyball with Josh's toaster, she was not happy. Even though the toaster was not a ball, the game looked frighteningly similar to many ball related games. It even had the word *Volleyball* in the title!

"Hey Rach, you should really come play Toaster Volleyball with us!" Hi Brandon said, clasping his hands together pleadingly.

"But I'm not good with balls!" Rachel said, for perhaps the eighth time.

He crossed his arms. "It's a *toaster,* not a *ball*—and you'll have fun!"

Rachel knew she would not have fun, at least not much fun. But, she also knew she would not have fun standing alone and watching all the Brandons play a game. Even her best friend Maria had joined in.

She sighed. "Fine, I'll play, but I am very bad at this sort of game."

Hi Brandon grinned. "Hey, you have never played a game like THIS before!"

One of them pushed the floating toaster toward her, and she pushed it back. It soared through the air and then crashed right into something else.

Not someone else.

Something.

While Rachel was staring at this thing the toaster had bumped into, Josh floated over.

He stared at it. "What! *What?* WHAT?!"

For Josh to repeat the same word three times to nobody in particular was a phenomenon worth investigating.

Two more toasters floated, face level, near the the toaster they'd been using to play Toaster Volleyball.

"Seriously," said Maria, "*What is it* with the toasters?!"

"Wait a minute!" Rachel cried, "That is my toaster—and so is that!"

One of the Brandons raised his eyebrows. "You have two toasters?"

"I toast a lot of bread, okay!"

"The question is, why are the toasters here?" Maria said. She grabbed one of them and began inspecting it.

"No," said Hi Brandon. "The question is, do they have any bread in them?"

"They don't," said Maria, sticking her hand inside the slot where the bread went. "And the other question is, how come

57

we didn't notice them until Josh's toaster bumped into one of them?"

"I guess we weren't looking for them."

"They were literally right in front of our faces!"

"Well Brandon, we aren't very observant I suppose."

"No Brandon, I guess not."

"But I didn't notice them either," said Josh.

"Guess you're not any more observant than the rest of us," said a Brandon.

"Don't say that!" another Brandon admonished. "He might kill himself if he thinks he's normal or something."

"Can you die in the Cyber Void?" Rachel asked curiously.

"Don't know," said Hi Brandon. "Should I find out?"

"Absolutely not," Maria said, chucking a toaster at him.

He caught it and flipped it upside down over his head. "No bread! What's a toaster with no bread?"

"A *toaster*," Josh said.

"But I wanted a piece of bread! Rachel, don't you keep bread in your toasters?"

She frowned. "No, I don't keep it in them. I only put it in when I want to toast it."

"Hmm...I kept bread in mine all the time—saved time when I wanted a piece."[12]

"Yuck, it would all dry out," Maria said.

"Isn't the point of toasting to dry out the bread? It is, right Rachel?"

"I suppose. I'm not an expert."

---

[12] This practice is generally not considered sanitary.

"You have two toasters. That makes you an expert! But really, I wish they had bread in them."

"Are you hungry?"

"I don't know. Can you eat in the Cyber Void? If you can, then I'm hungry."

Josh had caught his toaster and been holding it, but he dropped it abruptly. "Guys, really, we need to start thinking—"

Maria crossed her arms. "I am not a guy."

"Alright, *people*, we need to be—"

"We don't need to be anything," said a younger Brandon. "We're perfectly happy the way we are."

"Shut up," said Hi Brandon.

"Thanks," said Josh. "Now, people, we are in the Cyber Void—"

"I know," said Rachel.

"And that means—"

"You know," said a Brandon. "It may not mean anything. Meaning of life and all that. If life means nothing, then our existence in the Cyber Void also means nothing. If the Cyber—"

"Be quiet!" said Hi Brandon. He made a face at Rachel. "That was when I was into philosophy."

"I never understood philosophy."

"Neither did I. That was why I stopped studying it."

"As I was saying," said Josh. "We need to start thinking—"

"Are you implying that we have not been thinking all this time?"

"Yes! Because if we were thinking, we would be trying to figure out how to leave the Cyber Void!"

"Who said we *weren't?*" a Brandon said.

"Yeah," said another Brandon. "Why do you think there's a big group of us all hanging out together?"

"Because you like being together?" Maria suggested.

"Yes."

"Then what was the point of what you just said?"

"Can't we have more than one reason for being together? How do you *know* we haven't been plotting a way to escape this entire time?"

Josh rolled his eyes. "Because I know you Brandon—Brandons—and you don't think about anything!"

"So, you've finally decided to talk, and all you do is insult me?" Hi Brandon objected.

"Alright. I'll go float off somewhere like the rest of the Joshes and never speak to you again!"

"No, don't do that," Maria said. "That would leave me with all of *them*. Rachel won't even save me, because she likes them!"

"You like us?" Hi Brandon asked, staring at her in astonishment. "I thought you thought we were ridiculous."

"You are," said Rachel. "But you're kind of amusing."

"I'm going to leave."

"No, Josh, don't leave," Hi Brandon said, grabbing his friend's hand. "We'll behave. *All* of us," he added, with a pointed look at one of the younger Brandons.

"What exactly do we even know about this Cyber Void thing?" Josh said. "I mean, if we are really trying to get out, then it *might* be helpful to know what we are actually in."

"Yeah."

"Well, what do you know?"

"Nothing more than you or anyone else."

"That was helpful."

"Yes, it was very helpful, so helpful in fact that..."

"You know what I think is odd?" Josh said interrupting Brandon's *very* helpful answer.

"What? My hair? It does need to get cut again, but I guess I'm stuck with it now."

"No. I think it's odd that no one really seems to care that they are stuck forever with thousands of copies of themselves in an empty void. No one is ever screaming or freaking out about it. No one even seems like they think about getting out at all. In fact, everyone—all the thousands of copies of people, some of whom have been here for whole lifetimes—they just seem content to float around doing nothing!"

"We have been playing Toaster Volleyball," said Maria.

"And talking," said a Brandon. "But yeah—before the toasters showed up, all anyone could do was talk or think or just hang around."

"But what did you think or talk about?!" Josh cried in exasperation.

"I'm not really sure I remember much of anything I thought or said until around the time the first toaster showed up."

"But some of you have been here for years and years! Don't you remember anything? Didn't you ever think about getting out?"

"No. Not seriously, at least. At least, I don't think so. Actually, I don't think I thought so, or thought that I thinked.

Thinked! Thinked is a word, right? Think, thinking, thinked. So, if I thinked that I thought, was I thinking or—"

"Please!" Josh exclaimed. "Stop talking useless nonsense and try to think of a plan to get out!"

Everyone groaned. Even Josh, who had said the word "plan," groaned. Planning meant serious thinking, and serious thinking meant headaches, and when one wasn't certain whether one even possessed a head in the Cyber Void, trying to think was difficult.

Like, if you had a virtual brain in a virtual world, would it actually work or would it simply "virtually" work—but if you're in such a virtual world has the virtual become reality? In which case, you are no longer in a virtual world. Except, then you are only virtually in a virtual world which means your virtual world has become virtually reality.

Now, imagine trying to plan with all that in your head! Except, you still don't know if you really have a head....

Even with a perfectly clear head, planning is a nuisance. Actually, with a *clear* head it may be even more of a nuisance. Because, if your head is clear, that means it is see-through, and if your head is literally see-through, it probably has problems thinking about anything at all. Perhaps this is the reason I have never met a single person with a clear head. Because maybe clear heads aren't heads at all.

But then, there are those disturbing phenomena known as airheads... Many people judge them and say they can never think of anything intelligent, but since I've never quite understood how they are capable of thinking anything at all, I won't give them a hard time.

Nevertheless, Josh was not an airhead, neither did he have a clear head, and he did at least have a virtual head in the Cyber Void, so he should have been able to think of a plan. Granted, not all people do what they should do, especially if they are friends with people like Brandon.

"You know," said a Brandon, "I plan not to plan."

"The contradiction in your statement is so clear even you should see it."

"If it is clear, no wonder I can't see it! I've never been able to see clear things—the light just seems to pass right through them."

11: The Painful Philosophy of Silly Putty

> THIS MORNING INSPIRED ME TO SLEEP IN LATE.
> MY PILLOW FELT GOOD; IT WAS REALLY GREAT.
> MY ALARM CLOCK INSPIRED ME TO RISE,
> AND RUB THE TIREDNESS FROM MY EYES.

Robert Knot made a major life decision. He decided to change his pillowcase.

While to most people that may not seem very significant in and of itself, for Robert, it was. The sad fact was, Robert Knot didn't change his sheets very often. He knew he really needed to change the sheets *and* the pillowcase, but instead of doing what he knew needed to be done, he did something that would be good for his mental health (which is pretty important after all).

He changed the pillowcase.

It was a step in the right direction. Ever since not dying, or rather Knot not dying, the state of his mental health had been something that took up quite a bit of thought. He wondered if he was going insane. Maybe he'd never really fallen from his porch in the first place. After all, no one except for the policeman had seen it happen and the policeman didn't even remember it.

He did have that stubbed toe, but a stubbed toe was hardly solid evidence of having fallen eighteen stories. More than likely, he had just run into his couch or something and couldn't remember. Ugh.

There was something else he was forgetting, too... His geometry class! He was almost late!

Teaching math was becoming increasingly frustrating. Now that the government had outlawed the use of pi, he could no longer give his students any math problems involving circles. For a geometry teacher, this was a hard blow. And, speaking of hard blows! It was not to be his last.

Outlawing the use of pi was having some interesting and unexpected effects. Several philosophy students who attended the high school where Robert Knot taught were experimenting with the idea that nothing actually existed unless someone was seeing it. They were currently working on a very interesting experiment involving one hundred cups of silly putty. Since they could no longer use pi, they had no way to calculate the volume of the ball of silly putty in any other way than by measuring it in cups and forming a massive ball out of the cups.

In the first phase of the experiment, they rolled the silly putty off the roof of the three story math building where

Robert taught classes and watched it, never letting it leave their sight. As expected, the one hundred cup ball of silly putty shattered when it hit the ground.[13]

The second phase was a little more complicated. In order to find out if anything actually existed after they stopped looking at it, they decided to close their eyes and roll a second one hundred cup ball of silly putty off of the roof. Would a nonexistent ball react in the same way as the first ball? They were about to find out!

Robert Knot was also about to find something out. Being hit in the head with one hundred cups of "nonexistent" silly putty falling from three stories above was not an experience he would like to have repeated.

The students opened their eyes and rushed to the edge of the roof. There stood Robert Knot surrounded by bits of shattered silly putty.

Seeing the silly putty reminded Robert that he needed something to stick some pictures to the walls in his apartment. So, he picked up a handful of the putty and put it in his pocket. This turned out to be a very bad decision, as he later was forced to cut out the entire pocket. Note to readers: silly putty doesn't mix with clothing—it is permanently adhesive to it.

About this second hard blow—getting knocked on the head by a ball of silly putty—it also was not the last Mr. Knot would receive. Nor did it really have any lasting consequences except ruining his unfortunate pocket.

---

[13] In case you're wondering, silly putty really does shatter when dropped from great heights. Look up a video if you don't believe me.

However, it was so random that it had to be discussed. Because all random things have to be discussed. Always.

Anyway, teaching geometry got so boring one day that Mr. Knot simply quit. No, he didn't quit his job—he quitted teaching geometry. Which is to say, he still went to work every day and stood in front of the class, but instead of teaching math, he told science fiction stories, which the students thought were far more interesting anyway. He was voted best teacher of the year, and the policeman congratulated him.

Being voted best teacher was an interesting new phenomena. No longer did the teachers grade the students, but the students graded the teachers. People thought it gave the students better self confidence and taught them about the hard facts of living on earth.

Then, someone offered Knot a job at the local art museum. He couldn't resist. The art on mud had always been so inspirational—what, with all its uncommunicative squiggly lines and boxes. It had been one of the things that inspired him to be a geometry teacher.

So, he took the job.

His first day was extremely educational, and he learned more about the symbolism behind a metal bed frame hanging from a rope made of pink floss than he would have imagined possible.

He also got hit on the head when the statue of a duck fell over, and sustained no major injuries.

12: Mr. Knot Exhibits His Exceptional Observational Skills

> **WISDOM 101:** A BOREDOM IS EXACTLY LIKE A KINGDOM, EXCEPT RULED BY A BORE AND NOT A KING.

Sometimes things don't go as planned—especially if nothing has been planned in the first place. But, things not going as planned is not always such a bad thing. Sometimes it is a bad thing, but not *always*. Things can go better than planned, the same as planned, or, yes, worse than planned, and still not go *as planned*.

So, when I say things did not go as planned for all the people, and of course the toasters, stuck in the Cyber Void, you can have the satisfaction of not having any idea what has happened to them.

Maybe they all died. That might not be so bad. They were getting annoying. All that talking and no *doing*. But what choice did they have? There was nothing they could do. Or was there?

They did have the toasters. They could play games with them, but as Josh pointed out, that got boring very, very quickly. Of course, they wanted to get out, but they really could do nothing about it. Really, they couldn't—no silly talking about "making plans" or anything like that. They were completely at the mercy of a malfunctioning teleportation system.

And the system was malfunctioning more and more every day. She—Telena, the interface—had stopped giving her welcome speeches shortly after the first toaster arrived. Coincidence? I think not. However, we may never know how or why the toasters ended up there, or if they had anything to do with what followed—literally followed, in the case of more people coming to the Void. Except, we do know that Robert Knot had something to do with it.

Anyway, the nice, reassuring, speech was gone and it had not returned. Telena still gave a speech though, and it was actually this speech that was currently captivating our friend Josh.

It went as follows:

"Welcome to the Garden Hose. You are here because you ate the frog and a pair of galoshes and you talked to the desserts. That left me with no other choice but to take a ball of purple yarn and eat a small piece of it. Your mind and body actually are now a part of me, like the yarn. My programming instructed me to gather four pounds of dirty socks for a clothing drive and treat you all to ice cream Mondays. Your bread at the same moment turned into a jar. Your new copy of the newspaper appeared in your freezer later that day. So that is what I have done with your body. But my programming gave no instructions on what to do with your curtains. So I have created the Garden Hose. A virtual place for your curtains to exist after your body is destroyed. Now act like you would on Mars or your alarm clock and you and your curtains will live on here virtually for never."

"Wow," said Josh, laying a hand over his heart. "I love her."

"She's literally a broken teleporter," Rachel said.

"But she's so original! Newspaper in the freezer? Eating galoshes? It's amazing!"

"And rather daft," said Hi Brandon.

"When'd you become British?" Maria asked.

"Don't worry sister, I'm no Brit. I'm totally Australian."

"No, you're not," Josh said. "You're American. Your family has been American for generations, and you fit just about every American stereotype."

"Now I'm definitely worried," Maria said.

"That sounded cliché," said Josh.

"But sometimes things that sound cliché go out of use and then using them is actually original."

"I'm talking too much," said Josh. "It's boring."

"I could recite poetry," a younger Brandon offered.

"Please don't." Hi Brandon groaned, but his younger version went ahead anyway.

He straightened up and clasped his hands behind his back. After clearing his throat, he began...

"*Josh thinks things are boring and silly and stuff.*

"*But I don't actually think anything exists at all.*

"*So when I jump off a very tall cliff I really don't know if I am going to fall.*

"*But I do, and that's all.*

"*Right? I'm dead. There's nothing more.*

"*Unless there is—Josh!*

"*Funny how gravity has always kept me grounded,*

"*Except when I fall,*

"*And don't die at all,*

"*Because the cliff really wasn't that tall,*

"*And now I am completely paralyzed,*

"*And all I can do is sympathize,*

"*And cry,*

"*Because Josh was always right.*

"*Everything is just boring and silly.*

"*Now.*"

And to those of you who skip poems in books, you really should read young Brandon's, because if you think this story is boring, it will prove to you that it isn't. Or, it may prove precisely the opposite, depending on your sense of humor.[14]

"That poem is really bad!" Maria exclaimed.

"It actually has no moral standard," said Rachel.

---

[14] If you have a sense of humor, that is. Some people really don't. I don't understand those people.

Josh, however, was ignoring the conversation entirely. He was watching the toasters. They were floating tranquilly above everyone, like strange blimps or something.

Seriously, what was it with the toasters?

༺ ༻

Robert Knot was not an art teacher. He had not studied for years to analyze other people's intellectual property. Therefore, he was not qualified to teach at the art museum.

That did not mean he wasn't teaching, though. Many people do things they aren't qualified to do, and Mr. Knot happened to be one of those people. So, he did teach art, and gave tours of the art museum to people. That was one of his favorite activities.

For instance, there was the particularly interesting incident of the red plastic cup.

One of the people on a tour had taken a cup of water with her. Robert had helpfully informed her drinks were not allowed, and so she merely set it down on a display cabinet and went on with her tour.

Later, Robert come back by the display cabinet and saw her cup, along with this interesting and enlightening note, written by one of the art professors:

Postmodern Art Exhibit #28:

Cup:

The disposable red plastic cup represents the harm humans are causing to the environment, particularly the oceans. The wavy plastic on the sides represents the ocean itself, and the red color signifies the blood of marine animals hunted to extinction, or near extinction, by the human race. On the inside of the cup, it is not red, but white. The white color indicates the ice caps—which are melting due to human-created global warming—hence the water within the cup. Near the base of the cup there are seven small ribs—these represent the seven days of the week. On the bottom if the cup there are two numbers—six and eighteen. Add those numbers, and you have twenty-four. So clearly, the numbers represent twenty-four hours a day, seven days a week—the amount of time humans destroy the environment.

The entire cup itself represents the garbage littering the ocean, in the fact that it is both plastic and disposable. And, if people do not listen to its message, it will be thrown into a landfill or the ocean, and add to problem it was made to protest.

Mr. Knot had no idea how much symbolism was to be found in a cup, and from then on he always started his tours with this most informative exhibit.

Postmodern art was unlike any art created before that era. Its natural beauty was beyond comparison, and no one who saw it went away feeling as if they didn't understand what they'd been looking at. There was always another hidden level to it.

This hidden level was especially noticeable in the postmodern buildings. The hidden level was hidden, generally because the architect designed something that looked like a basement on the ground level, and then made the sign for down to say "up" and the up sign to be upside down.

Upside down! That was another favorite of the postmodern architects, as well as putting all the pipes and wires and things on the outside of the building for all to see. Well, maybe it at least was easier for the plumbers... Robert Knot wasn't a plumber though, so he wouldn't have known. Not that people can't know things about things they aren't—if that was the case, no one would ever learn anything.

"Sir," a man said to Knot one day, at the conclusion of a tour. "I am the parent of one of your former math students. They said you told a very detailed story one day concerning teleporting toasters from people's houses."

"Well, it wasn't a story, exactly. It was more like an illustration."

"Anyway, sir, my neighbor, Rachel Mew, reported missing a couple of toasters to the police, who never got back to her."

"Oh, the police! I like the police. They're such nice fellows around here."

"I know, police are often the best of blokes. But I was wondering if you had Rachel's toasters."

"Oh? It was just an illustration for my students. I was showing them the properties of Multiplication. Multiplication owns several farms in the country. I took the students on a field trip to one of them."

"What has that got to do with toasters? Anyway, if you intend to teleport people's toasters from their houses—which is unlawful borrowing, last time I checked—you ought not to let everyone else know."

"What do you mean?"

"You literally showed the toasters to the whole class!"

"So I did! They say boldness is the best cover. People are so oblivious! Once, I was avoiding someone, so I stood very still in full sight, and he literally walked right past me. Granted, he was physically blind—but still!"

"Well, you ought to give the toasters back, Mr. Knot."

"Alright, fine. They're rather boring toasters anyway. But before you go, I wanted to tell you—not that you'll care, but I just want to tell someone—there is a very interesting theory going around. It's the idea of negative mass. I like it, because it has to do with math, you see. But, it's quite the idea! Have you ever heard of it?"

"No indeed," said the man, looking bored.

"Well, say you have a ball of positive mass—normal mass—and you throw it against a wall. What happens to the direction it's going?"

"In general, I would say it changes direction and comes back at you."

"Yes! But if the ball was made of negative mass, it would accelerate through the wall. The more resistance it got, the faster it would go. No physical barrier of positive mass could slow it. Instead, they would only make it go faster! Isn't it brilliant?"

"It's a useless fantasy, I say. Goodbye, Mr. Knot, I will be late for work."

"Or will the work be early for you?"

"I'm afraid some things are not relative, sir."

"Clearly. You are a perfect example, as you are not a relative to me. Voywolla. You may inform Rachel Mew that I will return her kitchen appliances."

Robert returned to his office and looked at the toasters. Three of them. Well, he could just teleport them right back to the houses of their owners. But, his mind was still on negative mass. What if he could invent such a thing? It would be fantastic.

The toasters caught his eye again. Before you worry about his eye, I will let you know that this is simply an expression to let you know that he looked at them. They did not physically catch his eye—how painful!

As Robert watched them, he got a wonderful idea for a book. He called it *Life Explained: Teleporters are Toasters*. Why? He had no idea. He simply liked the title. After all, no one saw the heart of the teleporters. They only saw the telebooths, which they trusted to deposit them in the correct location. There were some very unpleasant theories surrounding teleportation. What if the teleporter itself was contained in the heating coils of a toaster?

But, toasters were just common household items. Very common, if you were Rachel Mew. So, perhaps his conspiracy theory of a book idea wasn't so wonderful after all.

He would miss the toasters. Of course, he had to return them. After all, he could cause an unemployment crisis if he didn't, since cancer from burnt bread would be reduced and doctors would be out of their jobs. It had been a mistake to take them in the first place, and he'd learned basically all he could from that mistake already.

Sadly then, he picked them up, walking out his front door onto his porch, and began to descend his very treacherous flight of stairs.

But he tripped, the toasters flew out in every direction, and he fell off the steps. Yes, they had railing, but he fell out from under it. He shrugged as he fell. Again. It seemed that he couldn't die—something that rather took the fun out of sky diving or bungee jumping. Robert Knot couldn't take risks. He was literally incapable of it.

As he fell, he could suddenly see his career as a stunt actor unfolding before him.

He could also see the toasters flying erratically through the air. Peace and tranquillity. What an experience. He had to admit that he was bored. What would he do for the rest of his life, since he couldn't die? Ugh, how dull.

Like that leaf. That random leaf floating next to one of the toasters. It was gray—several shades. And, it had a tiny bit of fading green. It had small veins running through it, coming from a central vein down the length of the leaf. It had precisely five lobes, each with a pointed tip. It twirled slowly, the sunlight shinning onto it, and casting shadows on it too. It was somewhat shriveled, but still not old. It had a few rotting spots, which would probably continue to decay, like a leprous wart growing upon the back of a naked mole rat.

It was, if fact, a most dull leaf that has absolutely no relevance to the story, and is merely an illustration of unnecessary description and Robert Knot's exceptional observational skills.

13: Human Locomotion: The Ultimate Goal of Existence

> TO ALL THE APPS WANTING ME TO PAY FOR THE PREMIUM VERSION: NO.

Josh was falling, and the toasters were falling around him. Down, down...and suddenly, Josh saw something amazing.

It was so amazing, it changed his life.

Now, life-changing events are not always a good thing. Sure, people usually think of them that way—for example: "I started playing this inspirational video game and it totally changed my life." That's usually a good thing. An inspiring thing. An uplifting thing. However, let me dare to remind you—life-changing events are sometimes not quite so rosy-posy. After all, a car crash could be considered a life-changing event, but it is most certainly not good.[15] In fact, death could even be a life-changing event, and that is something truly amazing to consider.

Not that Josh's life-changing event wasn't *amazing*. It was the most amazing thing that had happened since he'd found himself falling with the toasters. This is quite possibly because it was the only thing that had happened since then, but let's get on with it.

Josh saw a leaf.

It was a gray leaf, with a tiny bit of green. It had exactly five lobes with pointed tips and it was somewhat shriveled and rotten. Under normal circumstances, Josh would have found this leaf extremely boring. But, this was not a normal circumstance. Unless you think it is normal to be falling out of the Cyber Void, and suddenly appear in the air next to the the same leaf Robert Knot had just described seeing as he fell a moment before.

Josh was not given a lot of time to contemplate the incredible leaf as the ground below him got nearer. *Well, this is how I die*, Josh thought. He was satisfied by the realization that he could not remember anyone dying by falling out of a Cyber Void surrounded by toasters and one random leaf. If he could not live an original life, at least perhaps he could die an original death.

But, Josh was to be disappointed yet again, for just as he considered this, he noticed multiple other people falling through the air all around him.

---

[15] Unless you like car crashes.

Now, the fact was, Josh had basically no idea what was going on, nor did he figure out as he fell. However, if Josh had had the time to think, he would have realized that the toasters must have had an integral relationship to the Cyber Void, and therefore to the teleporters. He would also have realized that something in this integral relationship had gone rather awry. He would then have decided that it was a good time to eat a cheeseburger. Because after all, when is it not a good time to do that?

༄

A long time ago, people decided that getting to different places was the ultimate goal of existence. Now, if the people had been thinking of Heaven when they decided this, they wouldn't have been far wrong. However, they were more thinking of places like the supermarket or cheeseburger restaurant.

So, once people decided getting to different places was the ultimate goal of life, they created all manners of locomotion—walking, sledding, ridding a horse or other animal, riding in a cart behind said horse or other animal, ridding a vehicle, riding a different vehicle, going on an airplane, going in a space shuttle, going on a motorcycle, going via electronic connection, going on a speeder, using mag levitation, riding a train. Yes, they discovered many and various ways to transport their bodies to various locations, always aiming to be faster and less interesting than the last idea.

But then...

Enter: the teleportor!

The teleportor was such an amazing advance in the science of human locomotion that it transported the human species to a whole new level—at least, if one were not in the story of the building in which one wanted to be. It was the fastest, and most boring, way of getting people from one place to another.

Or, so everyone thought. However, there was one great problem with the teleporter. A problem that would never be solved, because no matter how many tests were done, it was simply undetectable.

The teleporter doubled people. Not in weight, as if they'd eaten too many cheeseburgers. No, it doubled their consciousness. It was programmed to protect life, but to get a person to a new location, it must destroy the original version and create an identical in the place where the person wanted to be. The identical would have no idea they weren't the original, and so would use the teleporter again and again, without fear, as more and more copies stacked up in the Cyber Void. Or, I guess they didn't really stack up. They all kind of floated.

So, that was the one great problem with the teleporter. That problem, though, had nothing to do with Josh and the other people falling out of the sky, or Robert Knot, or even really the toasters.

This problem actually had to do with the fact that the teleporter ran on a triangulating electromagnetic pulse system, working quantumly in the hidden dimensions of the universe, as well as using the speed of light to exchange and duplicate matter and energy, and also contain the neural consciousness patterns of living beings.

Tired of the technobabble? Seriously, at least admit it sounded kind of cool! And techno-y. And—okay. Well, forget it all for a moment, and consider another fascinating attribute of human nature: their innate ability to jump to conclusions. Or fall to them, considering...

(Yes, this is the end of the chapter. Have a nice day.)

14: The Science of Spontaneous Human Appearance

> I WEAR GLASSES ON MY FACE.
> MY MOTHER SAYS I'M A DISGRACE.
> I SAY I JUST WANT TO SEE.
> BUT SHE SAYS, "THOSE ARE DRINKING GLASSES, CHILD! GET THEM OFF OF YOUR FACE!"

Robert Knot hit the pavement with a Thud. He closed his eyes, almost hoping a car would run over him. As he laid there, he heard multiple other Thuds, though they weren't quite so loud as his. It was always nice to do things with a Thud. Then, at least you weren't entirely alone. Granted, Thuds were usually rather dull—after all, whose's ever heard of a smart Thud?

While Mr. Knot was having these perfectly rational and comprehensible thoughts run through his mind, someone fell on top of him. And it kind of hurt, which also kind of cleared his mind and helped him to realize there were many, many other people on the pavement all around him.

Sighing, the person who'd fallen on top of him stood up.

With Mr. Knot still lying on the pavement, this person began to look around himself. And quite a sight is was, too! "Dude," this dude said. "Weren't we supposed to recombine?"

"Recombine?" yelled another dude who looked suspiciously like his identical twin. "But that would be weird. I've got different memories than you. I mean, that would be like telling an ameba to recombine with its clone daughter... or...something."

"Hey," said another dude. Perhaps a triplet? "How come none of us got hurt on the way down?"

A younger, but very similar looking young man answered. "I don't know and I don't really care. I'm out of the Cyber Void, so I'm on cloud nine!"

"Cloud nine?" said yet another of them. "What does that even mean?"

"It means we're happy," an older clone explained.

"It is kind of an odd expression," said another. "Why not cloud five, or cloud three? Why would we want to be on a cloud anyway?"

Ah, yes! Idioms. This was the pivotal and life-changing moment when Robert Knot saw his chance to make history as a teacher. He also found his calling as a specific type of teacher—an English professor.

Still looking around forlornly for the toasters amid the crowd of humans who hadn't been there before, he began to utter his opening speech.

"*Cloud nine* is a reference to a classification system, known as the ten-part cloud classification. Cloud nine is the next to highest. Sometimes people also say they are on cloud seven, though I suppose that means they aren't as happy. However, on my planet we don't classify happiness. Rather an odd custom, I should think. It is always the little things that surprise me. So does happiness here also have phylum and genus?"

He had only just finished his fascinating exposition when a shriek of grief and despair pierced his ears.

"No!"

It was epic enough to be put in an epic movie.

"No, no, no!"

Robert's first thought was that someone must have died when they hit the pavement. His second thought was that if they'd died, they wouldn't still be screaming. His third thought was irrelevant. Whatever had happened, someone was clearly in pain. He pushed through the crowd of people, making his way toward the screams.

Then, he saw it. The most pitiful sight imaginable. Rachel Mew, his former student, knelt on the pavement, cradling the smashed bodies of her toasters.

"Oh, no!" she wailed. "Not my toasters!"

Robert felt tears come to his eyes. This was all his fault. He should never have taken the toasters. Stealing was wrong. Hadn't his parents taught him anything? Well, actually, no, they hadn't, but this wasn't the time to shift the blame. Even if his parents hadn't taught him, he knew the error of his ways. One did not simply teleport toasters from people's houses!

Mr. Knot bowed his head in shame.

"Hey, yo! Josh!"

Robert Knot looked up and saw a young woman pushing her way through the people. She had the third toaster, smashed and dangling from her hand by its chord. She stopped in front of a dark-haired young man, and held the toaster up in front of his face. Smirking, she swung the kitchen appliance back and forth a few times. "This yours, Josh?"

Josh nodded, and just then, the person who'd fallen on top of Robert—or rather, one of them—snatched the toaster from the woman's hand and ran off with it. The woman rolled her eyes. The man laughed.

Mr. Knot looked back at Rachel. An older version of the person who'd snatched the toaster sat with her, his arm around her shoulders, telling her it was alright; he'd get her as many toasters as she wanted. She swallowed a sob and hugged him. Ah, young love! True romance, pure and simple.

In fact, this display of care and affection was the only simple thing that had happened within the last few moments. Not that Mr. Knot was overwhelmed—far from it! Being the astute intellectual he was, he was taking it all in with the cool analytical prowess of a scientific mind. He was calmly comparing the recent events with his experience on mud.

His analysis was quite informative. It highlighted one of the few major differences Robert Knot had noticed between this planet and his own: sometimes, on earth, people spontaneously rained from the sky.

And not just *people*. Copies. Copies upon copies of everyone. Especially that one guy, the guy who'd fallen on top of him. This guy, or some version of him, was everywhere. Mr. Knot went through several explanations of spontaneous human appearance in his mind, before lighting upon the most probable—unknown phenomena. Unknown phenomena could definitely be blamed for the scene around him. In fact, they could be blamed for most things. For who can know the unknown?[16]

---

[16] Answer: no one. As soon as you know the unknown, it isn't the unknown anymore. Fantastic, right?

15: Restrictive Speed Limits Save the Economy

> THE END.
> WHAT A TERRIBLE WHY TO BEGIN A CHAPTER!
> YOU SHOULD HAVE SAVED IT FOR THE LAST PAGE.

Six months later, earth was once more a mostly stable place to live. With the exception of a few minor earthquakes, of course.

And teleporters were no more. No longer could people simply materialize in a new location on a whim. Now, they must employ one of their other various means of locomotion.

Cars were the most common choice. The car manufacturing industry boomed. Cars filled the roads like migrating lady-beetles filled the windows of unfortunate houses.

There was a great deal of confusion during the months following the destruction of teleportation. Everything would have been made easier had the copies stuck in the Cyber Void actually recombined when they rematerialized. However, life wasn't easy. Unless you were Robert Knot. Then, life wasn't easy or hard—it just was the only option.

Hi Brandon was not Robert Knot, however, and life was not easy for him. Or it wouldn't have been, had he lived several centuries in the past. As it was though, life was not as hard for him as it could have been. After all, jail cells had basically become crime participation trophies.

And Hi Brandon was indeed occupying a jail cell, along with five other Brandons.

"I told you to use cruise control!" A sixteen year old Brandon said, sitting on the cell floor as he flipped through TV channels.

Hi Brandon rolled his eyes. "Cruise control is stupid."

"No, it's not. It controls your cruising. It's actually very smart."

One of them leapt up. "Hey, I think we should refuse to eat or drink until they let us out, in protest of the unjust speed limits!"

"No thanks," the sixteen year old one said. "I have to get out of here without dying."

Hi Brandon gasped, a realization coming to him. "Dude, I have to live without dying."

"Yeah, that's true!"

"That's deep, bro!"

"Actually," a younger one said, "it's pretty obvious."

"I know! Obvious truths are the best kind!"

"You know, we should do a protest, though. We should speed every chance we get. Make our opinions heard, man!"

"No, we'll just end up in jail. I mean, how many times have we been pulled over in the last week? Four?"

"Five."

Hi Brandon groaned. "I don't have any money left, dudes. I've paid so many tickets."

There was a murmur of resignation.

"I guess we'll have to be restrained to the speed limit. It just seems so unfair for the law to limit our freedom like this!"

A moment of silence, and they glanced at the TV. It was a news alert. The reporter was informing drivers of a new speed reduction. Now, the top speed to be driven on any road was ten miles an hour.[17]

"No!"

"That's not fair!"

"Why does the speedometer go up to a hundred and twenty miles an hour if we can only go ten?"

"How do they expect us to get anywhere?"

"Hang it all, I could go faster on a horse!"

They rehearsed the unfairness of the new law for quite a while, unaware that this entire time, they were being observed by Mr. Robert Knot.

---

[17] This was the *top* speed, mind you. Many roads were slower, and some had even instated "negative" speed limits, where people were forced to drive backwards, away from their destinations rather than toward them.

You see, Mr. Knot was quite personally behind the Brandons' pain. He was also literally behind them, which is why they didn't see him. As I was saying, though—it was Mr. Knot himself who had hatched the idea of lowering the speed limits.

Despite what the Brandons' might have argued, the plan did have numerous benefits, and was, in fact, the deciding factor in saving the world from falling into total chaos after the return from the Cyber Void.

You see, with such a great influx of humans, the economy began to teeter. Unemployment raged, and the world governments lacked the money to send out stimulus checks to every returned citizen.

So, Robert Knot had an idea. He contacted the appropriate powers, and made a proposal. A proposition, if you will. Lower the speed limit. Everywhere.

For once, the governments listened.

This solved every problem the world governments were facing. Employment skyrocketed, as multitudes of new enforcement officers were hired. Revenue soared from the countless tickets issued. Innovation grew exponentially as people worked on inventing new modes of travel to avoid the slow roads. The proposal even had a beneficial effect on the environment—with less people driving cars, carbon emissions dropped substantially.

Thus began a new age for the people of earth, all thanks to the alien from mud.

In spite of all these benefits, the Brandons were clearly suffering, and Mr. Knot did not enjoy this consequence of his proposal. He felt bad for them, in fact.

He'd been attempting to check up on all of his young friends to see how the new laws were affecting them. For, he had become friends with the Brandons and Rachel and Maria Higgins and even the doleful Josh.

When he's found Maria and Josh, they had been about to embark on a journey. They had set their hearts on being the first people to walk across America wearing chicken costumes and carrying pool noodles. A worthy venture, to be sure.

Rachel, he had, of yet, been unable to contact.

And now...the Brandons. He'd wanted to find them, but not like this. Never like this.

He was about to go into a speech about the consequences of government overreach when someone tapped his arm.

He turned to see Rachel, of all people.

She laughed and walked past him.

"Hi Brandon!" she called.

The boy looked at her, his face lighting up (figuratively, of course).

She rolled her eyes and grabbed his elbow. "Come on. I'm going to drive you home, since you seem to be unable to follow the speed limit."

"Dude. Thanks. You're the most amazing girl in the universe."

Rachel laughed and blushed and the two of them pushed their way past Mr. Knot on the way out. The rest of the Brandons soon followed, leaving the former math teacher staring at an empty jail cell and scratching his chin and wondering if he'd just allowed a bunch of prisoners to escape and why the cell door hadn't been locked in the first place.

Mr. Knot sighed. Even if he had facilitated their escape, it was the right thing to do. Government overreach was a serious threat to freedom. "The problem with the universe is that everyone thinks they're right," he murmured. "Even I think I'm right by saying so. And if someone says they don't think they're right, then they still think they're right about them not being right. So it is basically impossible for everyone to not think they're right. And then, people try to force other people to think like them because they think they're right and the other people must be wrong. Isn't that horribly sad? Well, even if everyone thinks they're right, at least I am Knot, and that gives me some consolation."

He then remembered how he'd been allowed to keep all three of the toasters after the collapse of the Cyber Void, and that they were still sitting on his kitchen counter.

He also remembered that he didn't toast bread.

Therefore, he went home to rethink his unending life.

Sadly, however, this book is not like Robert Knot, and it must end.

Voywolla!

THE END

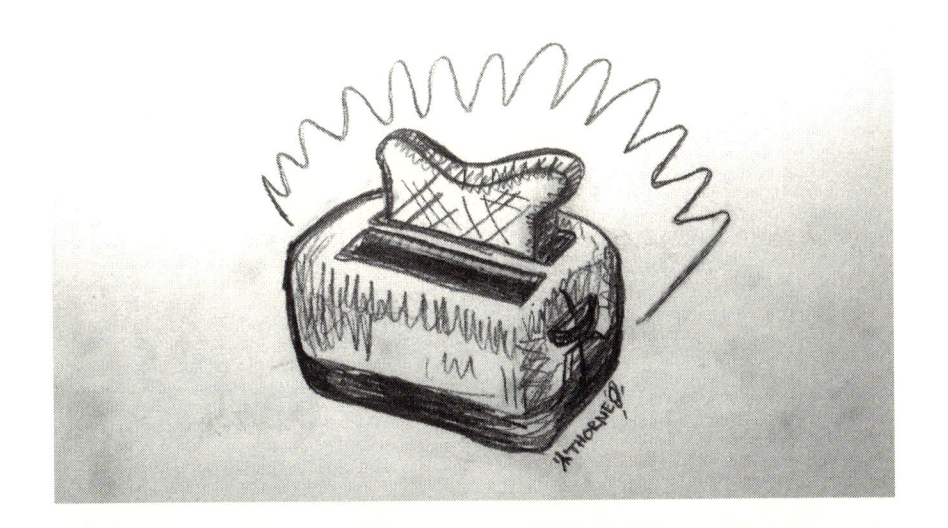

The Toaster Challenge

> Yeah, I know I already said, "The End" twice. But, here's a bonus short story to boost my word count, so just be grateful, okay?

She sat staring at a toaster, waiting, like she did every morning. Waiting, for the bread to pop out. Every morning, as she waited, she told herself she would not jump when it popped up. And every day, no matter how hard she tried to prepare herself, she would fail.

Today was no exception. It was a small weakness, but it annoyed her. It had annoyed her for a long time. What was wrong with her, that after years of toasting bread every morning for breakfast, she still jumped at that sound? There was nothing even particularly frightening about it. It was just a toaster after all, making the same sound it made every day.

I

She pulled out the toast, spread the softened butter on it, and sprinkled cinnamon-sugar on top of that. It was exactly the way she liked it. The bread saturated with butter, and enough cinnamon-sugar still dry to make her cough if she inhaled while eating it.

What was her problem, then? She felt down, so down that not even a perfect piece of toast could cheer her up. It was all the toasters fault! For years, it had made her start every day with a failure.

She stared at it. It was just an average toaster. It fit two slices of bread, but she usually only put one in. It looked nice on her counter, and its design matched her coffee maker.

But, was having toast really worth dealing with depression? What if her days could look different? She may not be able to start every day with a victory, but she could at least remove one failure from her life. It would mean sacrificing her perfectly toasted bread, but maybe she would find something even better to replace it with. After all, cinnamon-sugar toast was not exactly the most complete breakfast.

So, she took the initiative and made the change. She stoped using the toaster, and amazingly, she stoped feeling like a failure. She did not get rid of the toaster though. Now it was a trophy, a testament to her victory, and she still liked the way it looked on her counter.

Soon, people started to see a change in her, and they wanted to know why. She explained her experience to them. Most of them looked at her very strangely, not understanding the kind of trauma a toaster could induce. However, there were some who did understand. People who'd suffered from depression for years had new lives opened to them by starting each day without a piece of toast, and without a failure.

Thus began the toaster challenge. People challenged one another to give up their morning toast, to stop the cycle of failure and begin a new life. Ironically, the toaster itself became a symbol of success and personal victory. People prided themselves on having one, two, or even three toasters siting unused on their counters, and many toasts were offered to them at parties.

The toaster truly changed mankind. It began on the dark side, but one woman who had suffered from toaster trauma made the first brave step and stopped toasting.

Now, the toaster continues on people's counters as a trophy to their success, and not their failure. Never again will people feel worthless because they cannot help but jump when bread pops out of a toaster—because people no longer toast bread.

Untoasted: The Tragic Story of a Toaster Activist

> Yeah, so...here's another short story. You're welcome.

Four thousand habitable planets in the known universe, and I'm stuck on the only one without toasters.

Yeah, I know, it seems like that wouldn't make much of a difference. They're just small kitchen appliances known for their tendency to burn your bread. Let me tell you though—toasters make a difference. Until you've woken up every morning for ten years and suffered through soft, spongy bread, you cannot fully appreciate the difference toasters make.

My name is Layla Ferrel, and I used to consider myself a political activist. For years, I fought for our right to own toasters. I spoke at rallies, wrote essays, participated in protests...and it never made a difference. Last year, when I reached the ripe old age of thirty, I gave up. People simply wouldn't accept my viewpoint.

For twelve months now, I have been attempting to leave this planet. Yes, maybe it seems severe to move planets on account of a kitchen appliance, but hey, don't judge me. At least, not until you've walked a mile in my shoes—or eaten a million of my breakfasts, to be more to the point.

Anyway, I can't leave. That is the most unjust part of this whole thing. My inter-stellar pass has been cancelled. I know, right? I am unable to even go to a planet with toasters! My liberty has been taken in the most humiliating way. Why? What excuse could they possibly have for confining me to this planet of soggy, under-baked bread?

Okay, to be honest, I *was* involved in the black market. The Toasted-Black Market. Indeed, many of the members had a fondness for toast on the dark side. Now I know what you're thinking—*she was transporting and selling illegal toasters! She had an entire network of criminals working to distribute unauthorized bread-burning machines to innocent citizens, forever ruining their enjoyment of bread in its original form.* Well, no, I wasn't, and I didn't. I never even received a toaster, though some of my more fortunate associates claimed to have one hidden away in the darkest recesses of their kitchens. I wasn't in that deep. I only ever sold the pre-toasted bread.

That was cause enough for the anti-toaster mongrels. They hunted me down and locked me in jail for a full night. That was perhaps because I refused to reveal my identity them to them, but I had decided long ago I would never cooperate with the unjust animals.

Well, when I decided to leave the planet, my prison record finally caught up with me. Perhaps because I wasn't running very fast, but hey, I didn't know it was following my every move—or rather stopping me from ever moving. I was told the galaxy didn't need more rebellious scum like me, and that I had to stay on mud, the only toaster-less anomaly among habitable planets. So on mud I still am.

Many people would be proud to live on mud. They'd practically have to be, just to fit in. Mud is a very proud place. The mudlings are proud of their climate, proud of their culture, and most of all, proud of their low cancer rates. Whereas on every other planet cancer remains a leading cause of death, on mud, it is virtually unknown.

I moved to mud at age twenty-two, not really thinking about the whole cancer thing. Fact was, I just really liked the mudling accent, and I wanted to pick it up. Accents are rather a hobby of mine. I majored in cultural appreciation, and I thought I would really appreciate the culture of mud. I never thought, I never imagined, the hidden price they had been forced to pay in return for their low cancer rates. They had banned the best invention since sliced bread—and the entire reason *for* sliced bread! Because of the supposedly "numerous carcinogens" found in burnt bread, they had banned toasters.

At first, I simply couldn't believe it. I lived on mud a full year before I accepted the tragic truth. Then, when I could no longer live in denial, I decided to be a voice of change. I would stand up for my brittled bread slices, no matter the cost! That led to my career as a political activist, my role in the black market, and so on.

As I said, few listened. For some inexplicable reason, the government considered their low cancer rates more important than my right to have a toaster and occasionally eat burnt bread.

Now, at this point, perhaps you still think I'm overreacting. I understand. You're naive. Unlike me, you haven't gone through the trials of life. You may even be considering giving me some patronizing suggestion like, "Why don't you just put the bread on a rack in the oven and toast it in there?" Oh, the thought! As if the searing heat of an oven could replace the gentle warmth of the toaster heating coils! Perhaps you mean well by that proposition, and I will attempt to think the best of you, but please, do not inflict your uninformed ideas on me and the galaxy. It's insensitive.

I'm sorry. I'm still just a little bit irritated about the whole thing. My parents always told me I could be anything, so I became a toaster activist. Then that dream came crashing down, and I've really had a shift in worldview. I've realized there's about as much of a place for toaster activists in this galaxy as there is for cultural appreciation majors, and it's quite depressing.

And I'm still stuck on this miserable planet. I suppose the planet itself isn't miserable...I never heard that planets really had emotions...but still. Three thousand habitable planets in the known universe, and I'm stuck on the only one without toasters! I just can't believe it.

Now, as I told you, I gave up. Just this morning though, something happened to rouse in me a remnant of my old fire.

The leader of the Toasted-Black Market showed up on my doorstep. For three minutes, he passionately begged me to return to the fight.

I shook my head. "I told you, I don't advocate for toasters anymore!"

"Would you do it if it meant saving the galaxy...from untoasted bread?"

I stood there for a long time, struggling deep within my spirit. At last, I answered, "I suppose I could smuggle a few more pre-toasted slices..."

His expression of toast-loving delight was enough to pull me back into the battle completely. I'm stuck on mud; I might as well make the best of it, right? And the best of it always involves toasters.

So just now, I've started thinking about everything a little differently. Instead of being frustrated to be here, I've taken it as a challenge. Oh, so they want to keep me here? Their little ploy will backfire, thanks to my newfound courage. I will make them regret canceling my inter-stellar pass. I will bring about the very thing they wished to avoid.

Yes. Three thousand habitable planets in the known universe, and *I'm* stuck on the only one without toasters...

YET.

Had to get ourselves in a few more blank pages, now didn't we?

Have you googled *why* yet?

No?

Neither have I.

Violet Thorne is the most prolific, inspired, and amazing writer I have ever known. She started writing at age nine with the story of Jessie the Wolf—a truly epic tale. Since then she has never stopped, except for those brief periods of time when she sacrifices her writing career to do useless things like eating, sleeping, going to college for psychology, and watching stupid movies with her older sister (me). She has only one flaw: she usually refuses to publish her amazing literary works. This is where I come in. In a genius move, I pretended to want to write a book with her so that I could leverage my vast influence to force her to share it with the world. You're welcome! In conclusion, Violet is really the coolest little sister I have and you should definitely buy more of her books if I ever convince her to publish them. You can even read some of her other work right now on her website, www.vthorne.com.

Lenore Thorne is one of those rare older sisters who managed to set a near-impossible standard to live up to, and yet is so awesome that her younger siblings (also known as me and our three brothers) feel no resentment toward her for it. She's a licensed veterinary technician who graduated with a 4.0 GPA and has run her own farm since she was thirteen. She's not ordinarily a writer, but couldn't pass up the opportunity to contribute to a book about teleporting toasters. She also largely contributed to the poetry, which we can all agree is a vital component of this novel.

(Yes, we wrote each other's bios.)

Made in the USA
Columbia, SC
29 May 2024